D1557739

TALBOT MUNDY:
MESSENGER OF DESTINY

TALBOT MUNDY:
MESSENGER OF DESTINY

Compiled by

DONALD M. GRANT

DONALD M. GRANT, PUBLISHER, INC.
WEST KINGSTON, RHODE ISLAND
1983

CONTENTS

Page

INTRODUCTION by Donald M. Grant   9

AUTOBIOGRAPHY   15

WILLIE—ROGUE AND REBEL by Peter Berresford Ellis   27

TALBOT MUNDY by Dawn Mundy Provost   75

GHOSTS WALK . . . by Darrel Crombie   115

TALBOT MUNDY IN *ADVENTURE*   121

THE GLORY OF TROS by Fritz Leiber   171

BOOKS   175

MAGAZINE APPEARANCES   217

THE JERUSALEM NEWS   245

THE THEOSOPHICAL PATH   249

THE NEW YORK TIMES   253

TALBOT MUNDY
MESSENGER OF DESTINY
1879-1940

*I have failed often at what I at-
tempted, and at the time I have
learned from failure nothing except not to flatter it by calling it the
end. At its worst it is but a beginning of some new phase of destiny.
But looking backward, as when
remembering night at daybreak, I
have learned what gives me courage to look forward. I perceive that
failure more often than not is the
fruit of a man's forgetfulness of his
own importance in the Eternal
Plan.*

From the Log of
Tros of Samothrace

INTRODUCTION

It is not exactly politic for an editor-publisher to acknowledge that he has a personal favorite among writers, but for a good many years now I have made no secret of my admiration for the writer generally known as Talbot Mundy. (Happily, I am not alone in this admiration — as evidenced by the flood of contributions from a score or more of bibliophiles who responded excitedly when they learned of an impending Mundy bio-bibliography.) Three books — the two lengthy volumes that make up the "Tros" saga, TROS OF SAMO-THRACE and PURPLE PIRATE, along with the Oriental masterpiece, OM / THE SECRET OF AHBOR VALLEY — remain to this devotee of the unusual the finest fiction I have ever been privileged to read. There are others: THE DEVIL'S GUARD, OLD UGLY FACE, CAESAR DIES, and KING— OF THE KHYBER RIFLES. I don't pretend to say that this latter quartet of titles equates the remarkable qualities found in those three favorites first named. But they are exceptional works from an exceptional author; a most unusual man!

However, the purpose of this volume is not to evaluate Mundy's writings. It is to present the facts of bibliography, along with other basic materials which I hope will provide a new understanding of this unique man and, in turn, prepare the reader for a full-scale biography later this year from the pen of Peter Berresford Ellis. Enough to say that the writer's extraordinary ability with the pen was enough to inspire me to look beyond his books.

Information about Talbot Mundy — at first glance — seemed fairly abundant, and a mimeographed bibliography by Bradford M. Day, first published in 1955, already existed. Biographical and autobiographical sketches revealed that Mundy had been born in England in 1879, was educated at Rugby, and at an early age went off adventuring to Germany, India, Africa, and Australia before settling in the United States in 1909. His first published story was "A Transaction in Diamonds" in the February 1911 issue of *The Scrap Book*. His first work in *Adventure,* beginning a long and glorious association with the magazine that printed countless thousands of his unforgetable words — both fiction and non-fiction — was "Pig Sticking in India" in the April 1911 issue. His first book was RUNG HO!, published by Charles Scribner's Sons in 1914. But once beyond a certain level of knowledge, facts came with increasing difficulty. A trip to the city of Manchester in the neighboring state of Connecticut during the late 1960's revealed a house on Pitkin Street in which Mundy had lived — along with the startling information that he had written the old radio serial, *Jack Armstrong: the All-American Boy,* for the last five years of his life. Not so startling, I decided, on reflection. *Jack Armstrong* had been a part of my childhood in the late 1930's, and the mixture of wonder and adventure (the show often stretched beyond the bounds of probability) was one of the initial influences in my lifetime love affair with the fantasy genre.

But there, the trail petered out.

I began to wonder why. It was almost as if Mundy's background were as elusive as the mysterious "masters" he wrote about. The thought occurred to me: "Could Talbot Mundy be a pen name?"

In October, 1976, I received a letter from the British author, Peter Berresford Ellis, who also writes fantasy under the name of Peter Tremayne. Peter Ellis was unknown to me at this time, and the subject of his letter is long since forgotten. Certainly it bore no relation to Talbot Mundy or to his writings. But, at that time, Peter lived on a thoroughfare in London called *Chetwynd* Road, and that in itself was enough to prompt a query in the form of a postscript to my reply: "Do you know anything about the British-American author, Talbot *Chetwynd* Mundy?" Now Peter knew and admired Mundy's writings — possessed rather a modest collection of his books, as a matter of fact — but he could offer next to nothing about the man's personal life. Yet it was that query that eventually opened the floodgates of knowledge about Talbot Mundy.

An obscure, penciled notation in the register of Rugby School led that remarkable literary sleuth, Peter Ellis, to the discovery that Talbot Mundy had been born William Lancaster Gribbon! The transformation turned out to have been anything but orderly — as you will learn — but from that point on, fact followed fact with astonishing rapidity. Shortly thereafter, literary agent Kirby McCauley was kind enough to affect an introduction to Mundy's agent, and subsequently a meeting with Mundy's widow, Dawn Mundy Provost, was arranged. Happily, both Dawn and Peter Ellis were persuaded to join in the building of this volume, and their contributions, for which I am most grateful, go far beyond the articles contained here. In addition, Peter has gone on to complete the writing of an extensive biography of Talbot Mundy to be called THE LAST ADVENTURER.

Contributions in the form of articles soon arrived from authors Darrel Crombie and Fritz Leiber, and the major collectors of Talbot Mundy began to peruse their libraries for little-known information. Among this group was Charles N. Brown, editor-publisher of the esteemed science-fantasy journal, *Locus,* who put his marvelous collection at my disposal. Charlie also supplied most of the dust wrapper photographs reproduced in this volume. Great assistance was also provided by the "old tiger," Dr. Darrell C. Richardson, who has collected Talbot Mundy for more than forty years, in that time becoming one of the foremost pulp experts in the world. Charles Ford Hansen of Denver, Colorado, another large collector, marshalled the Mundy collectors of the Rocky Mountain region and made his findings available to me. Charles Schlessiger of Brandt & Brandt, Mundy's agent, provided the materials toward a bibliography that had been compiled by the late bibliophile, William J. Clark, and Charles' quiet encouragement did much to insure the completion of this volume.

I am most grateful to these individuals and to the following for other valuable assistance and contributions in the compiling of this work: John B. Akin, Robert N. Alvis, Robert Booth, Walter A. Carrithers, Charles Cockey, Charles Collins, L. W. Currey, Paul Dobish, Lloyd A. Eshbach, William Evans, Major General Nigel St. G. Gribbon, Roy Hunt, Louis Lambert, Roger Luedemann, David E. Mann, Kirby McCauley, Sam Moskowitz, the late H. Warner Munn, William Peacock, Elliot K. Shorter, Paul Spencer, Oswald Train, Richard Wald, Robert Weinberg, and Robert K. Wiener; and to a quintet of librarians: Edgar Bailey and Paul L. Bazin of Providence, John Bell of Ottawa, William Durow of Cedar Rapids, Iowa, and Roberta Hankamer of Boston.

I am also indebted to Mr. W. Emmett Small of Point Loma Publications, San Diego, California, for permission to repeat the inscription found in Katherine Tingley's copy of OM / THE SECRET OF AHBOR VALLEY, to the Lilly Library of Indiana University, which houses the Talbot Mundy/Bobbs-

Merrill correspondence, to Mr. Bill Balgey of Popular Publications, Inc., for the use of material pertaining to Talbot Mundy in *Adventure* magazine, and to the publishers The Bobbs-Merrill Company, Cassell Ltd., Constable & Co., Ltd., Doubleday & Company, Inc., E. P. Dutton, Inc., the Hutchinson Corp., and Charles Scribner's Sons for permission to reproduce dust wrapper illustrations of Talbot Mundy books.

October 1982

Donald M. Grant
West Kingston, Rhode Island

TALBOT MUNDY:
MESSENGER OF DESTINY

The autobiographical sketch of Talbot Mundy that follows first appeared in the April 3, 1919 issue of Adventure *magazine. It was preceded by two short introductory paragraphs from editor Arthur Sullivant Hoffman, who revealed that it had been written some five or six years earlier, and "because of those famous 'exigencies of space' " did not find its way into print until 1919.*

AUTOBIOGRAPHY

It happens very seldom in a man's life that he gets the opportunity to talk about himself to the people who are going to read his stories; and it happens still less frequently that he can do it without his victim's being able to talk back. So I'm going to make the most of this. Sit still, and suffer!

Why shouldn't a man talk about himself? I know when I read a story I always wonder whether the writer of it has lived through the fear and the joy and the various mixed emotions that he portrays, or whether he is only guessing. If I know that he has seen it all, or something very like it, I enjoy the story; otherwise I don't. And I dare say I am not at all unusual in that respect.

Standing at my own grave-side, and looking down into the grave that had been dug for me, was what actually started me at the writing game. Though I did not actually begin just at that time, it put the notion into my head that some of my experiences might make valuable copy. I made the usual beginner's mistake at first of writing the bald narrative of what had happened, instead of inventing new episodes and fitting men I had met into them.

Naturally nobody wanted to read the unvarnished experiences of a rolling stone, strung into paragraphs but quite devoid of plot; in fact the only excuse for talking about them now is to prove that I know more or less what I write about, for a man who has knocked about the world for fifteen years or so without getting rich has very little to boast of.

But I was born with a thirst for adventure, or at all events I developed it at a very early age; and along with it came an insatiable passion for finding out how people would act under given circumstances. For instance, one of the earliest things I can remember is sticking a pin into a man to find out what he would do; and what he did to me was a very small matter when compared to the satisfaction of finding out something for myself.

My people destined me for the church or the law, I forget which, but I know they gave me the choice of two evils and that I chose a third that they never even dreamed of. They cut off supplies to enforce obedience and I went without supplies — to Germany. The method of choosing my destination was my own idea, though I have no doubt that many people have used it before and since; but it is so delightfully simple and devoid of detail, and I have used it with desirable results so frequently, that it is worth mentioning.

The plan is to first count all your money and then, by consulting railway time-tables and shipping lists, to find out just how far it will take you in any direction. Then put just so much of a map of the world on the table as your money will cover, shut your eyes and make a jab at the map with something sharp. Make a note of the town or village nearest to where the pricker lands, and go there without further argument. My pricker landed on a place called Quedlinburg in the Harz Mountains, and I arrived there a couple of days later with an English five-shilling piece in my pocket, a fox-terrier dog on a leash, and a portmanteauful of clothes somewhere on the line behind me. I have often wondered who got the portmanteau.

There was a sort of mechanic person in Quedlinburg just then; his job was driving a traction engine that towed some vans belonging to a circus. He talked tolerable English, and, as I couldn't talk German, I was glad to make friends with him. He had only two ambitions. One was to keep his job, and the other was to get drunk — very drunk, and very often. I helped him to satisfy one of them the first night with my five shillings. The next morning he gave me a job. In future I was to drive the engine and he was to drink the beer; I was to get ten marks a week from the proprietor and eight more from him, but on the other hand I was to do all the work, take all the blame if anything went wrong, and sleep under the engine in all weathers, so as to be "Johnny on the spot," so to speak.

It turned out to be a good job, and I liked it, and I found out all there was to know about that traction engine in a very short time. We had a steam roundabout and swings and boxing-booths, and some wild animals in cages along with the circus; in fact, it was almost a traveling fair. My job at night was to drive the dynamo that was fixed on to the front of the engine, and I used to sit up on the driver's seat and watch the crowd and absolutely revel in the noise and glamor and confusion.

But one day my mechanic friend got more than usually drunk and killed my dog; and he got the worst of the battle royal that followed. Of course that ended our gentleman's agreement and I had to quit; and I tried my luck from end to end of Germany after that, working at any sort of job I could get, and usually hungry.

I got a good job at last — back close to Quedlinburg where I started. But it seems that in this extraordinary world a good job always has a handle to it; you've got to give your whole time and thought and energy to your boss. I was hired distinctly on those terms, and I made good, but I didn't like it. A man back in England happened to hear that I had made good and hired me at a salary that was absolutely enormous for a boy of seventeen, but on absolutely the same stipulation.

My new employer had a peculiarity that is not at all uncommon among men of his type in England; he loved buying expensive hunters, but he had not always the nerve to ride them; so quite a large part of my duties consisted in riding his hunters for him three days a week or so during the season. Besides being splendid sport and keeping me in excellent condition, the experience gave me a knowledge of horsemanship and wood-craft that has been invaluable since. I piled up money, though, because I hadn't a chance to spend it. As a matter of fact I piled up too much money, and that, and the fact that I was barely twenty-one and that my job had grown monotonous, got me going with the map of the world and the sticker again.

This time, though, I could afford steamboat fares, so I hadn't got to cut the map. I had the whole wide world to choose from at random, and the compass point came down bang in the middle of India. I asked my employer whether he hadn't any kind of pull that would secure me a job in that country, and, as good luck would have it, he had; he secured me a sort of hybrid Government job in a Native State, and I started off for India feeling something as Alexander must have done.

The first thing I saw in India was a bullock-cart loaded up with corpses

— legs and arms sticking out from every side of it, and a fetid mixture of flies and aroma floating up above. That looked good to me; I thought that maybe I might really get interested before long, and I left Bombay with a heart full of hope and a boxful of Kipling's books in the railway carriage with me. Plague, of course, was the cause of the corpses in the bullock-cart; they were on their way to be disposed of at the burning-ghat; and, though I hadn't bargained for it, I had to spend the next fifteen months fighting plague and cholera and famine in turn — single-handed a good part of the time — in a temperature in the shade of anything from one hundred and twelve upward.

The only compensation that made the job in anyway worth while was the pig-sticking; that, and fox-hunting, are the two finest land sports in the world, and I got nearly all I wanted of it, though I could not always get away. There was a sort of permanent tent club not far away; it was the one common meeting ground for the white men scattered through the district, and when the morning's sport was over and we were lounging under the double flies I had the privilege of talking to some of the most interesting men I have ever met — men who were giving up their lives out of absolutely unselfish devotion to their country.

I found out no end of things of course, and it was very interesting, but I can't say that I enjoyed it. No doubt the impression that the experience made on me has come in very useful since, but I don't like to think about the details for very long at a time; the sight of all those thousands of people, good decent people, too, for the most part, rotting to death from various causes and suffering unspeakably would be likely to have a sobering effect on any one. The worst part of it was being able to do so little for them.

I went down pretty badly from malaria and overwork, and a sort of temperamental nausea, so when the plague had retired under cover and the famine had lessened sufficiently to give the Government time to breathe, I asked to be relieved, and another man was sent to take my job. I could have had another job straight away had I wanted it; but I had a sort of notion that I had been deep down into hell, and I had no desire just then to take the trip again. The prospect of a trip to Europe with a pocketful of money was much more alluring, and off to Europe I went to luxuriate and loaf and breathe clean cool air for six months.

But six months of Europe are enough for anybody at one time, and I soon got hungry for India again, for, after all, I had seen only a little corner of it, and that from only one point of view. This time I was lucky enough to arrange with a big firm of publishers to act as their occasional correspondent, and I walked on board the P. & O. steam at Tilbury docks with the idea firmly planted in my head that I was going to set the Thames on fire at last. I didn't do it, of course; but I had a durned hard try.

A little native war broke out almost directly after I landed, and on the strength of the credentials I had with me I hadn't very much difficulty getting to the front as a sort of junior war correspondent. My word! When I walked out of the Government office at last with the signed permit in my pocket I wouldn't have traded jobs with anybody in all the wide world! I could see fame in the offing already, and fortune coupled to it. Even now I would rather make a reputation as a war correspondent than in any other way, so you can imagine what I felt like then with what looked like the chance in front of me. I remember I felt awfully sorry for all the unfortunate writer-men who hadn't got my opportunity.

But I started in to make a whole lot too much of the opportunity. The thing wasn't so good as I thought it was anyhow, and besides that I was much too keen. The General commanding the British forces was enjoying his first experience of the war game too; he hadn't felt his feet yet, and he didn't believe in war correspondents on any terms; but he particularly didn't want anybody there to criticize him during the early stages of the campaign. Of course his objection was perfectly natural under the circumstances, but it didn't suit me; he issued an order forbidding any one to leave the lines after dark, or at any time without permission; and as he never once gave his permission I disobeyed the order. Or, at least, he said I disobeyed the order.

What actually happened was this. I kept pestering him for permission to visit the advanced posts, and he kept on refusing; and each time he refused he did it more violently and with less command of his temper. At last one afternoon I was particularly insistent, and he turned round and told me to "go to ————!" Well, I took that for verbal permission to go just where I pleased; a fellow can't go to ———— until he knows where it is, and I set out to find it.

I didn't get back to camp until two hours after dawn the following morning because a Ghoorka picket happened to hear me, and they amused themselves by firing volleys at me at intervals from midnight onward, and I had to wait until the mist lifted and they could see who I was. I hid behind a rock, but they made awfully good shooting in the dark, and chipped pieces off the rock all around me. Even when you know you can't be hit, the experience of being fired at is not pleasant, and it is still less so when you are wet through and shivering with cold.

So I lay there and tried to console myself with the knowledge that I had secured some quite important information. It was important, too, because the General pumped me dry and made use of it. But he didn't say thank you. He censored my despatches out of existence, and ordered me back to the base for disobedience to orders. And back to the base I had to go, having seen both the beginning and the end of my career as war correspondent within a month.

I went tiger-shooting after that; and then on a trip up to Afghanistan, though I hadn't gone very far over the Himalayas before the Government turned me back. I had come to the conclusion by that time that the Government of India was a pretty difficult outfit to fool, so I had a look at China and Singapore and the Straits Settlements and gave them time to forget me. I thought that wouldn't take long. Then I took a trip up the Persian Gulf on a tramp steamer with a black skipper; we broke down half-way up the Gulf, and then I really did know what — — — — was like. On that trip I saw oxen being fed on dried fish. It sounds improbable, but I saw it with my own two eyes.

I cooked up a gorgeous scheme then for a trip with another man up through India to Siberia, but the South-African war broke out and that put quite another complexion on things. Of course I hadn't seen anything like the whole of India; a man couldn't do that in a life-time. But I had seen and got to know Tommy Atkins at his best, and the men who lead Tommy Atkins "when the guns wheel into line," and my head was already cramfull of facts and fragments of facts that have since formed the foundation for such stories as "The Phantom Battery." If I have the ill-luck to live a hundred years, and keep on writing all the time, I may be able to exhaust half the stories that I know I can write about India; and though I have dived down deep into it, and seen it from several points of view, I know no more of it than a crab knows of the ocean. India is some country.

I wasn't tired of it yet by any means; in fact I have always meant to go back there again some day; but for the present there was a real live war to go to, and there were quite a lot of men in India besides myself who imagined that war was the one big picnic that should on no account be missed; so we made quite a strong regiment. We spent our own money on accouterments, and landed in Africa with only one regret among the lot of us — that it wasn't going to be a real war. It seemed to us an awful pity that such a fine regiment as we were should be wasted on a coconut-shy campaign against an enemy that hadn't any cavalry. We were cavalry — to begin with.

Barring a few prisoners, and mighty few of those, I never saw a live Boer the whole time. The picnic consisted for the most part of lying in the rain and being fired at, or lying in the scorching sun and being fired at. The rations were usually dead trek-ox or dead horse, dry biscuit, nice green water to wash it down with, and as a general rule no salt. There was no smoke to speak of, but every now and then you could see a flash somewhere on the hillside in front of you, and sometimes the man next to you would give a short sudden sob and lie very still. Or then again, sometimes he would sit up and scream, and go rolling over and over in agony. When the ground wasn't wet it was swarming with vermin, and most of the men who weren't shot went sick either from the vermin or the flies or the bad water or else exposure. I had the good luck to get hurt with a piece of shell before the relief of Ladysmith, and that meant Cape Town for me, and nothing more to do.

The people in Cape Town who weren't talking treason were all full of schemes for getting suddenly rich. I thought out a scheme too. So two months later I left Cape Town, broke to the world and very glad indeed to get a job before the mast on a big steel sailing ship. I did the same thing again not long afterward, but not from choice, and I have since left off wondering why men can be found who are fools enough to go to sea at all — I mean on merchant ships. We were short-handed, fed on offal that would not be good for pigs, ill-treated, struck, sworn at, overworked all the time, housed in a fo'castle that was swarming with rats and vermin, deprived of any kind of privacy, and, in fact, treated like animals. Only animals are never worked so hard.

By the time that we reached Australia another Englishman and myself had had enough of it, so we ran away from the ship, leaving our kit and our wages behind us. We neither of us had any qualifications that were likely to get us a job up country, but we hadn't any money either, so we couldn't stay in Sydney; we had either to walk or go to sea gain. We walked.

The two of us tramped all the way to Brisbane together, asking for work at every place we came to, and never getting it. We got food, though, because in Australia they have to feed all "sun-downers," as hoboes are called; if they didn't, nobody would ever go on the road to look for work. Now and then we eked out a little money by singing songs in wayside pubs, but we arrived in Brisbane just as broke as when we set out.

There seemed nothing else for it but the sea again, and we finally reached

Hobart, Tasmania, in the stokehold of a small steamer. The work was hard, but the grub was good, and the pay (ten pounds a month) was quite excellent. Hobart is a lovely little place, but I couldn't see any chance of getting rich there. Charlie (the other fellow) elected to stop, though, and I pulled out alone, before the mast again, on a three-masted barque loaded up with blue-gum piles for the new pier at Delagoa Bay.

There is no need to describe that ship; it is sufficient to say that she was worse than the first one. We were very nearly wrecked on the way across, and the crew went sick from being fed on salt fish; every man Jack deserted, including myself, at Lorenço Marques.

Lourenço Marques is a pretty easy place to go broke in; and when you are broke it must be nearly the hardest place in the world in which to get on your feet again. Before I succeeded in getting a job I got so low with fever, and so absolutely busted, that I was glad to accept the hospitality of a Chinese laundryman; he put me to bed between clean sheets, and fed me back to health again. Then he told me where to go and get a job! I landed the job at the first try, and it was a good one, too, if you reckon without the climate.

I had to run a big estate up the Limpopo River, and while doing it I am glad to say that I was able to help my friend the Chinaman. It seems that he was getting too prosperous, and the local officials came down on him for an extra big rake-off. He refused, so they trumped up two or three charges against him and put him out of business, fining him every cent of money he had and turning him out on the street penniless. Then he remembered me, and one day he arrived at my hut on the bank of the Limpopo, much more dead than alive. It was turn about then; I gave him a bed and fed him back to health, and then lent him money, and in about three months time he was in a fair way to becoming a prosperous trader, buying corn from the natives and shipping it to the coast.

Then I went down with fever so badly that I had either to chuck my job or die, and, not being at all anxious to die, I did the other thing. The British East African Government had just finished the railway to the Lake, and the country was being boomed like wild-fire, so I decided to go there and took the very first steamer with the idea of getting well again on the way up. Of course everybody knows now that British East Africa is a very much over-rated country; there is neither mineral there nor anything else of much value except wild game; but I was one of the comparatively early birds who helped to find it out.

There were no jobs to be had, but there was some money to be made shooting elephants, although one had to ignore the Government regulations in order to do it. Off the beaten track, though, it was not very difficult at that time to keep out of the Government's reach; the job was to slip through into the open and, once outside the pale, to stay there until you had cleaned up what you were after. So I hired a native named Kazi Moto, who had just come out of jail, as my personal servant and took the train up country. Kazi Moto means "Work like ————," and he certainly did fill the bill. With his help I got a *safari* together and slipped through into the elephant country, where I joined a Greek of most blazing amazing courage but very doubtful reputation.

The hunting that followed was the hardest and most dangerous work I ever tackled; for excitement it beat war all to smithereens, and among other things it gave me an insight into the meaning of the word fear. I will take off my hat at any time to a man who can truthfully say that he is not afraid of a charging elephant.

I didn't get rich at the game, but I made enough money to pay my men and I got hold of a good big mob of cattle, which I drove down over the border into German country. A marauding band of Masai tackled me not far from Shirati and drove off the whole lot. Naturally I resented it and, in the process of doing so, I received a spear-wound in my right leg. Kazi Moto killed my assailant with the butt end of a gun and then proceeded to suck my wound. He said he was sucking out poison and that he wasn't sure that he had got it all out. I didn't believe him, but he called up six other of my men, and among them they threw me on the ground and cauterized the wound thoroughly with firebrands. During the proceeding I bit Kazi Moto, who was sitting on my head, rather severely, but he never bore any malice about it.

The cattle being my only visible wealth and the cattle being all gone, all my men except Kazi Moto ran away, taking their loads with them in lieu of wages; and Kazi Moto and I set out to reach Muanza, a place nearly two hundred miles away, where the nearest doctor was. By the time I reached there I was naturally about all in, although, but for the fact that it was full of insects, my wound was not so bad as might have been expected.

The Germans were not at all pleased to see me, but, as I had developed black-water fever, they gave me a place to go away and die in. It was a dark and very dirty shed with a grass roof, which, besides me and Kazi Moto, had to shelter nearly all the rats in East Africa. Kazi Moto used to go out every day and steal things for me to eat, and once a day the doctor would come, look at me, give me a bottle of physic, grunt and go out again.

One morning he brought a sergeant with him and I heard him say to the sergeant, "All right . . . he'll be dead by this afternoon . . . you'd better send the chain-gang over to the burial-ground and get his grave dug, then we can get him out of the way before dark."

He didn't come in that morning, but just looked at me through the door; what he said to the sergeant, though, did me more good than all his physic. Up to that time I had not particularly wanted to get well; I had neither money nor prospects and was feeling much too ill to care, and I haven't the least doubt that if he had said nothing I would have died either that day or the day following. But I hated the man so, and was so utterly disgusted with his treatment of me, that I made up my mind to disappoint him, and from that minute I began to get better. When the chain-gang came with a sack to tie me up in I was sitting up with the aid of Kazi Moto. Two days later I leaned on Kazi Moto's shoulder and walked out to have a look at the grave; I was so weak that I very nearly tumbled into it.

Until then it had never once occurred to me that I had found out nearly enough for a young man of my age; but, looking into it, and back across it, I realized that, although I had done absolutely nothing to be proud of I had really acquired quite a lot of information. I sat there for about an hour, thinking; and at the end of it I pushed some dirt down into the grave as a sort of concrete sign that I had buried the old wanderlust at the bottom of it and would try henceforward to put my garnered knowledge to some use. I have not wandered more than twelve or thirteen thousand miles since.

I did a good bit of trekking about German East Africa after I got better, but this time always with a view to making money; and when I found that I could not make more than enough to live on, I decided to go up to British East again. So I took passage on a dhow, and that was another choice experience. The dhow was about thirty-five feet long over all and was loaded down with cargo. The cargo was covered with a sort of thatched roof, under which, and on top of the sacks of peanuts and drums of ghee, I and Kazi Moto, two native women, two babies, two goats, some chickens and eleven other natives including the crew had to exist. The voyage lasted ten days and it rained in torrents the whole time. When we made a smudge to drive out the mosquitoes the smoke was intolerable, and when we threw the smudge overboard the mosquitoes swarmed in like a hungry army.

One night the native who was sleeping next to me died (of pneumonia I think); I felt his back getting colder and colder but I had no idea that he was dead until the morning. They carried him ashore, and buried him in my blanket.

I did all right up in British East, for I secured a road contract, and, when I made good on that, the Government gave me an official job. But the climate where I was was awfully unhealthy; I had made up my mind by that time to write stories, and I had to work too hard to be able to find time for writing. In addition to that, people had a distressing habit of committing suicide there; they did it one after another, and that kind of thing gets on your nerves after a while.

I saw two native campaigns, but they weren't sufficiently exciting to make up for the depressing surroundings during all the rest of the time. A final dose of black-water fever convinced me that I had had enough of Africa, so I paid off Kazi Moto and sailed for Europe. Before I left, Kazi Moto stole my razors, watch, camp-kit and some of my money, but I don't grudge him any of it. I had intended to give him everything except the watch, so he didn't get much more than he was entitled to anyhow. He was a good man, and he saved my life four separate times.

Europe turned out to be as amusing and as comfortable and as unsatisfactory as ever when I got there. So I held the map and used the pricker. Others maintained that I made it come down in the U.S.A. on purpose. At all events I am glad that it did so.

Now that's a deuce of a long talk about very little, isn't it! But I've left a whole lot out. What I've tried to do is to prove that I've met real live men and seen them behave under all sorts of conditions, and that I've suffered with them and seen what they've seen and laughed with them sufficiently to be able to understand them and their motives. And consequently I claim that the people in my stories are real people who are worth writing about.

That is the only claim that a writer-man has any right to make. He himself, his private life, and his present possessions are matters of absolutely no importance; but his experience does count, because that is his only qualification, barring of course the technical knowledge that he can learn at school.

It goes without saying that there are different sorts of experience which are suitable for different styles of writing. Mine has been mixed and varied, and I try to write various stories. I have dined with a prince, who was afterward a king, and also at a Chinaman's table between my host and a buck Zulu; it doesn't matter which experience I liked best; the point is that I have sampled both. I have earned my living carrying sacks of potatoes at the wharf-side, and I have also had a very good time indeed in certain London clubs; and in between those two walks in life are an unnumbered host of others, many of which I have come into contact with at one time or another.

I claim to be nothing but a lineal descendant of the old-time story-teller, who spun his yarn and passed the hat round. Nowadays it is the editor who passes round the hat, and he is rather more particular than the old-time capper used to be; but the effect is just the same. The public pays, and the public calls the tune. I believe, too, that the public likes to know now, just as much as it did then, that the man who spins the yarn has seen the things he writes about. I have no other excuse for discussing myself and my wanderings over so many pages.
Talbot Mundy.

WILLIE — ROGUE AND REBEL
Talbot Mundy: The Early Years 1879—1909

by Peter Berresford Ellis

Against all fear; against the weight of what,
    For lack of worse name, men miscall the law;
Against the tyranny of Creed; against the hot,
    Foul creed of priest, and Superstition's maw;
Against all men-made shackles, and a man-made Hell —
    Alone — at last — unaided — I REBEL!

That verse, taken from Talbot Mundy's first book RUNG HO!, is expressive of Mundy's early life and attitudes from the day, aged only sixteen, he ran away from home rather than obey his family's wish that he be educated for a career as an Anglican minister. That rebellious streak followed him throughout his adventurous life and continued in the development of his later career as one of the highest paid[1] bestselling authors of adventure-romance both in America and the United Kingdom.

To the end of his life Talbot Mundy remained an extremely intriguing and complex individual, living the life of a personality which he had created, with a name and a past which were only loosely based on actuality. In interviews and articles, Mundy told stories of his early life which were mainly pure invention. The truth is that had Mundy told the truth about his early life, the most ardent of his fans would have dismissed it as too unlikely even to constitute the plot of one of his most imaginative adventure novels.

In a way, what appears is two different men: — the rogue and rebel of the period prior to his arrival in the USA in 1909 and the successful writer and raconteur of post 1909. Most adherents of Mundy's works know the latter but it is the former that this essay is concerned with.

Talbot Mundy was born on April 23, 1879, at number 59 Milson Road, Hammersmith, which was then a residential suburb of London. He was the eldest son of a chartered accountant named Walter Galt Gribbon and Margaret Lancaster. The proud father went to register the birth of his first born child with the local registrar, William C. Crofts, on May 16. The name he was given was William Lancaster Gribbon and he was formally baptized in the Anglican faith in the local church of St. Matthews on May 31 by the curate W. W. Archer. To his family, William Lancaster Gribbon became affectionately known as Willie and, even today, it is Willie they remember rather than Talbot Mundy.[2]

The Gribbon family can trace their roots back to 16th Century Ireland where the name derived from an Anglicised distortion of an Irish name *Mac Riobin* or Robin's son. The name was first recorded in 1511 A.D. and said quickly with an English pronunciation it became Crebbin, Cribbin, Gribben and Gribbon.[3] The name is still popularly found in the north of Ireland while the Crebbin version of it is commonly associated with the Isle of Man. Family tradition, however, has it that the Gribbons came to England with William the Conqueror and were Norse in origin. One branch of the family supposedly crossed to Ireland with the Anglo-Norman invasion of 1172 A.D. while another branch settled in Lancashire. The Gribbons had a strong military tradition in the family going back several generations to an ancestor, James Gribbon, who fought in the Napoleonic Wars in the 40th Regiment of Foot.

Willie's father, Walter Galt Gribbon, was born in the city of Leeds, Yorkshire, on May 29, 1845, and was the eldest son of a china and glass merchant named William Gribbon, after whom Willie was named. Walter Galt went to St. John's College, Oxford, in 1864, obtaining a Bachelor of Arts with a second class degree in jurisprudence and modern history four years later. He received his Master of Arts degree in 1871. In the meantime, on October 8, 1866, he enrolled as a student at Gray's Inn, one of the famous London inns of court, to study law. He was never called to the Bar but he does not appear to have relinquished his membership of the Gray's Inn Society and, therefore, technically he remained a student until his death. He appears to have displayed a talent for his studies for, in 1871, a report in *The Times*[4] records:

> ... the annual prize amounting to £25 (an exhibition [award] founded by Mr. John Lee QC, Ll.D. late Bencher of the Inn) for the best essay selected for this year upon the following subject: — 'The Feudal Tenures; their Origin, their Nature, and the Causes which led to their Abolition' was awarded to Mr. Walter Galt Gribbon, a student of the Society.

Walter Galt Gribbon (1845-1895). Talbot Mundy's father, whose names "Walter Galt" he used as an early pseudonym.
(Courtesy of Maj-Gen. Nigel St. G. Gribbon)

By 1871, Walter Galt had given up any ambition to become a barrister and had gone to Swansea, in Wales, where he started a career as a schoolteacher. On September 5, 1871, Walter Galt Gribbon married twenty-three year old Catherine Agnes Holroyd from Byfleet in Surrey. Her father, James Holroyd, described his profession as 'gentleman.' The marriage took place at St. Mary's Parish Church in Byfleet. Soon after, Walter Galt moved his teaching job to Wimbledon, then in the county of Surrey, and he and his wife moved into Tabor Cottage, Tabor Grove, Wimbledon.

Tragedy soon overtook the couple and on November 22, 1874, Catherine was taken ill and died of 'enlargement of the heart with dilation.' Walter Galt was present at the bedside of his young wife when she died.

Not long afterward he gave up his job as a schoolteacher. In 1877 he entered accountancy and became an associate member of the Institute of Chartered Accountants on July 21, 1880, while working in the Wool Exchange in the City. He quickly established himself as a popular and successful member of his profession and on February 4, 1885, he became a Fellow of the Institute of Chartered Accountants.

On July 3, 1878, Walter Galt Gribbon married again. At this time he was living in Byfleet, the village from where his first wife had come. His second wife was Margaret Lancaster, aged twenty-five years, the eldest daughter of Sam Lancaster of Nantyglo House, Nantyglo, Monmouth, in Wales. The ceremony took place in the Anglican Holy Trinity Church at Nantyglo. As Walter Galt had been living and teaching in nearby Swansea before he married his first wife, it is possible that his acquaintance with the Lancaster family had started at that time.

Sam Lancaster's settlement in Wales was only a recent one. The Lancaster family were a very old English family who claimed to trace their descent back to John of Gaunt, the son of Edward III of England. Sam Lancaster was one of seven brothers and seven sisters and the family was a fairly wealthy one which had risen to prosperity in the industrial north of England through the acquisition of ironworks and coal mines. In Nantyglo, Sam Lancaster was the managing partner of Messrs. John Lancaster & Co., the family firm, which owned the local colliery and iron works. He was a prosperous and well respected businessman and also a local Justice of the Peace.

A brother, Joshua, had gone to the United States in 1887 and remained there until 1894, living mainly in the south where he had established several business enterprises.

The most famous of the Lancaster brothers was John, active in Sam's firm, who was a Liberal Member of Parliament for Wigan from 1868 to 1874 and won historical fame as the rescuer of the captain and some of the crew of the Confederate American warship *Alabama*. The *Alabama* was the most famous of the ten Confederate warships built in Britain during the American Civil War. These warships were a great threat to Federal forces and successfully raided northern shipping in the Gulf of Mexico and the Atlantic. *Alabama* was built at the Laird Yards at Liverpool and in June, 1862, having been launched in the River Mersey, sailed to the Azores where she was fitted out as a warship. During the next two years, under her captain Raphael Semmes, she was responsible for the capture and sinking of 65 to 70 Federal ships.

In June, 1864, *Alabama* was undergoing repairs in Cherbourg when Captain John A. Winslow in the USS *Kearsarge* appeared off the French coast. The *Alabama* decided to leave Cherbourg and fight. A crowd of 15,000 gathered at the harbour to witness the historic battle, among the spectators was the painter Manet who painted a remarkable picture of the scene. The *Alabama* was outgunned and sunk.

The *Kearsarge* picked up seventy survivors, French boats picked up a further ten survivors while Captain Semmes and another forty crew members were picked up by an English pleasure yacht, the *Deerhound*. It was owned and skippered by Talbot Mundy's great-uncle John Lancaster.[5] In spite of protests from the *Kearsarge*, John Lancaster took the survivors to England rather than hand them over to the Federal American ship for imprisonment. It was not until 1872, after years of international wrangling, that Britain finally agreed to compensate the Federal Government to an amount of $15 millions for losses inflicted by the *Alabama*.

A member of a later generation of Lancasters, who Willie knew, became a U.S. citizen and chief of battleship design at the Norfolk Navy Yard, Virginia. Willie wrote to his younger brother in 1937:

> One of the Lancasters called on us the other day and brought a son-in-law with him. We liked them both. Lancaster is the chief of the battleship designing department at the Norfolk Navy Yard. He came over here when he was quite young and has been a citizen for more than twenty-five years. He is a quiet chap, who had never returned to England and doesn't intend to. He agreed with me in being one hundred per cent in love with the U.S.A. . . .[6]

Margaret Lancaster Gribbon (1853-1913), Talbot Mundy's mother.
(Courtesy of Maj-Gen. Nigel St. G. Gribbon)

Walter Galt Gribbon and Margaret Lancaster were married by the Reverend J. Morgan, MA, and, following the customary "wedding breakfast," the couple left Nantyglo on the 1:30 p.m. train for Bristol where they changed trains for the coastal resort of Ilfracombe, Devon, where they spent their honeymoon. The Gribbons returned to London where they moved into the house in Hammersmith where their first child, Willie, was born the following year.

Willie was joined by another brother, Walter Harold, born on January 29, 1881, and called Harold to distinguish him from his father. On July 3, 1882, a sister Agnes Margaret was born and promptly called Daisy.

Walter Galt's accountancy business was becoming very successful. From 1880 he had moved into his own offices at 5-6 Great Winchester Street, EC 2. By 1890 he formed a partnership with Archibald Brown Ingram and the partnership was joined by Barron Dennet Holroyd, the brother of his first wife, soon afterwards. Ingram left the partnership in 1894. With the business thus expanding, the Gribbons left the tiny terraced house in Hammersmith in 1883 and moved to a more luxurious house called "Belmont" in Clifden Road, Norbiton, then just outside of the extreme southern suburbs of London. At "Belmont" a fourth child, another daughter, was born called Florence Mary. The birth took place on October 22, 1883, but the child died when less than a year old on August 29, 1884. Soon afterwards, the Gribbons moved again, this time into a spacious house called "Combe Lea," in Gloucester Road, Kingston Hill, Surrey. The new house was not far from "Belmont" and, it seems, that Walter Galt kept ownership of "Belmont" for after his death his widow moved back to this house.

Walter Galt was now an established, successful businessman; a director of the Woking Water and Gas Company Ltd., a prominent member of the Conservative Party and treasurer of the Kingston Branch of the Primrose League (a Tory pressure group). He was also a devoted Anglican Church layman and senior auditor of the English Church Union.

When the Gribbons moved to the Norbiton-Kingston Hill area they found that the parish was a large one and the parish church of St. Paul's was too small to adequately serve the area. Walter Galt threw himself into a movement agitating for the building of a new church. The result of this agitation was that on June 5, 1883, the Bishop of Rochester went to Kingston Hill to open the new church of St. Luke's, off Elm Road. And it was an old friend of Walter Galt's the Reverend George Isaac Swinnerton MA, who had been a fellow student at Oxford, who was transferred from his curacy at Emmanuel Church, Streatham, to become the first vicar of the new church. Describing the official consecration of the church, which did not take place until December 14, 1889, the *Kingston and Surbiton News* records:

> A handsome lectern of brass, of light and elegant design, the desk being supported on a slender stand rising from a triangular frame, has been given by W. G. Gribbon MA. This gentleman has not only been of the greatest service to St. Luke's in the capacity of minister's warden, but he has rendered valuable help to his brother collegian (the Rev. G. I. Swinnerton) by reading the lessons in church.

As church warden of St. Luke's, Walter Galt was enthusiastic as he was active and the local newspapers of the period, *The Surrey Comet* and *Kingston and Surbiton News,* are full of references to functions, meetings and other activities attended by Walter Galt and his wife. Reverend Swinnerton later paid Walter Galt this compliment:

> For many years one name stood forth among the friends of St. Luke's, of one who was the church's friend in the early days of the old building; and as was often the case, he found time in the midst of his own busy life to help on that body which carried the message of Jesus Christ. When he (the bishop) was anxious to build a church, the one person who helped him most was a great businessman, who said that it was his recreation. The work bent the bow the other way, and Sunday was the great refreshment of his business life. So it was with Walter (Galt) Gribbon, to whom that night they dedicated the pulpit.

The pulpit in St. Luke's, of carved oak, still carries a brass plaque in memory of Walter Galt, which was erected by the parishioners; and the brass lectern, donated by Walter Galt, is still in use in the church.

It was against this strict Victorian middle-class background, with its strong accent on church life and conservatism both in religion and politics, that the seeds of Mundy's, or rather Willie's, rebellious character were beginning to take root.

The home life of the Gribbon children was, apparently, a happy one. Every summer Walter Galt and his wife would take Willie, Harold and Daisy on holiday to an English seaside town, usually on the south coast, such as Sandgate or Hythe in Kent or Charmouth in Dorset. Even in later life Willie recalled those holidays. "I remember Sandgate where we had the whooping cough," he wrote to his brother, "and the barracks at Shorncliffe and the hotel at Hythe."[8] And, again to his brother, "I remember Charmouth. I have a very vivid recollection of a boot shop run by a funny old lady who wasn't quite right in her head. I also remember a partridge that flew against, and broke, a bedroom window. Even to this day I hate like hell the scoundrel who picked up the partridge, stuffed it into his pocket and walked off with it. The hell with him!"[9]

Sometimes the three children would be sent by themselves to spend the long summer holidays with an uncle and aunt at Bardney, in Lincolnshire. Rachel Lancaster, a younger sister of Margaret, had married a prosperous landowner named William Hubbard Sharpe who had a large agricultural estate at Bardney, ten miles east of Lincoln, which employed six hundred people. The Gribbon children used to have enjoyable holidays on the estate which are still remembered by their cousin, May Sharpe.[10] Of Willie she can still recall:

> We all loved him, and he used to do all sorts of fascinating things. Once he took me to a fair and we went on the swings and he swung us so high that I was almost paralysed with fear. But he instilled trust in everyone.
> I remember we had a Stilton cheese which became old. My father used to soak it in port. Willie became tired of this and buried the cheese in our garden. Then he wrote a poetical epitaph on it and presented it to my outraged father. Alas, the poem is now lost.

One of Willie's earliest memories was of the death of his maternal grandfather, Sam Lancaster, when he was four years old. Sam Lancaster died on November 14, 1883, at the age of fifty-four. The body was taken from Nantyglo, in Wales, by train to London where it was buried in Highgate Cemetery. A South Wales newspaper[11] reported:

> All through Nantyglo and Blaina the whole of the shops were closed. The funeral was one of the largest ever known in the district. The coffin was placed in the hall of Nantyglo House and was viewed with evident sympathy by hundreds of workmen. Shortly before 3 o'clock the funeral courtege

started from Nantyglo House . . . all along the route, upwards of three miles, there were evident indications of the respect and esteem in which the deceased was held.

The chairman of the Nantyglo Ironworks Co., paying his last respects, said that Sam Lancaster "was the life and soul of a great many of the good movements in the Valley, and we feel his loss, I assure you, very acutely indeed."

Years later Willie wrote: "Isn't Highgate the cemetery where grandfather Sam Lancaster was buried? I have a vague recollection of having visited Sam Lancaster's grave when I may have been about eight years old, perhaps younger. It seems like a mental picture of Highgate Cemetery. A very dismal place, especially if raining."[12]

Willie's other early memories were of being timid.

> . . . I was born timid. As a child, I was in terror of a barking dog; to me, a horse was a thing of sheer horror, and a ride, even in the front of my father's saddle, a strong arm holding me, was torture. Fortunately, I had a grandfather who understood and began to teach me, at the age of four, that the purpose of life is to learn to be manly and that our wits are given to us for that purpose.[13]

The only grandfather alive when Willie was four years of age was Sam Lancaster for his paternal grandfather, William Gribbon, had died on September 26, 1866. As Sam Lancaster was dead by the time Willie was four years and four months old, one wonders just how much Willie really remembered about him.

> Fear of dogs was easily overcome, and so was the dread of snakes and darkness. I have never become a good horseman, although by the time I was sixteen I was not afraid to ride to hounds; in fact, I found it much easier to force myself into dangerous situations than to learn the difference between common sense and cowardice. I grew afraid of my own self criticism and killed one good horse under me rather than surrender to fear of an almost impossible jump over posts and rails, with a ditch on the near side, that a fearlessly sensible man would have avoided.[14]

Willie also recalled:

> . . . I was born with a thirst for adventure, or at all events I developed it at a very early age; and all along with it came an insatiable passion for finding out how people would act under given circumstances. For instance, one of the earliest things I can remember is sticking a pin into a man to find out what he would do; and what he did to me was a very small matter when compared to the satisfaction of finding out for myself.[15]

In a correspondence with his editor at Bobbs-Merrill, Hewitt Hanson Howland, Willie said that he had not read much as a child. Nevertheless, in another letter, he asked Howland "Do you remember Q's *Dead Man's Rock?* It was my boyhood's chief delight!"[16] But it seemed that Willie delighted more in listening to stories. He recalled that it was his father who had told him the basis of the tale he eventually worked into "The Soul of a Regiment." And there were other storytellers who used to frequent the Gribbon household who must have left an impression on the young boy.

One uncle, Blakely Gribbon, adventured in Australia and eventually died at sea. Another uncle, Pat Gribbon, died in Tigre while exploring Argentina. An aunt, Anne Gribbon, became a missionary and was reputed to be the first white woman to explore Lake Tanganyika. Yet another aunt, Kathleen Gribbon, married a clergyman, and became a missionary with her husband in Africa.

The family doctor, a close friend and neighbour, was a rather flamboyant Irishman named Doctor Nathaniel Henry Kirkpatrick Kane. Kane never ceased in delighting to tell of his fascinating adventures. He had been born in India and was ten years old when the Indian Mutiny broke out, a setting Willie was to use in many of his later stories. Kane and his parents returned to Ireland where he matriculated from Dublin University. As a doctor he served with the Red Cross during the Franco-Prussian War of 1870 and was decorated several times for his services in the field. He then took to the sea, as a ship's doctor in some of the P & O ships, before settling down in Kingston. Like his friend and neighbour, Walter Galt, Kane was a staunch Conservative, active in the Primrose Club, the local Anglican Church and various other local bodies. He died from pneumonia on Thursday, October 22, 1896, leaving a widow and four children all under the age of ten years.

Another friend and business colleague was a young man named Curwen

Sisterson, who had left school at the age of fifteen to become an apprentice in a merchant firm in the City. In an amazingly short while Sisterson became chairman of the firm. He toured South Africa, Zululand, the Transvaal and Central Africa, investing wisely in gold mines and other business enterprises. He became a Fellow of the Royal Society of Literature, stood for Parliament as a Liberal candidate in the General Election of 1892, became an urban district councillor and chairman of his local council, was a Justice of the Peace and a member of the London Scottish Volunteer regiment. Yet he was still only thirty-eight when he died in 1899.

In February, 1895, he had married Mrs. Sadie Spaulding of New York at St. George's, Hanover Square, London, with the ceremony performed by the Bishop of Lichfield. Willie's sister, Daisy, was the bridesmaid and a newspaper reported:

> ... the youngest bridesmaiden, little Miss Gribbon, looked very sweet and dainty in a cream-coloured frock trimmed with lace and ribbons, and a white velvet hat set with white ostrich plumes; she carried a basket of flowers, mostly daffodils.[17]

School came as something of a shock to Willie Gribbon. He was sent to a preparatory school which he bitterly recalled when filling in a publisher's publicity questionnaire in later years. It was, he said, "a school at Guildford where an inferiority complex was regarded as righteous and yelling was a medium of instruction, a rotten cane the method of stirring affection."[18]

The school was called Grove House, later Boxgrove School, standing on the corner of Boxgrove Road and Boxgrove Lane in Guildford, Surrey. The school was founded by F. S. Pridden MA, who was its first headmaster from 1882. He appears to have ceased to be headmaster in 1905 for, in 1906, H. F. Caldwell and D. MacLachlan are reported to be jointly in charge of the school. Perhaps its most famous pupil, in the 1920's, was Christopher Robin Milne, made famous by the poems of his father A. A. Milne. The school seems to have been closed in the late 1930's.

In spite of Willie's memories, he appears to have been a good pupil. His family still retain a volume of *Ingoldsbys Legends* (widely known through H. Rider Haggard's Allan Quartermain tales as the only book, other than the Bible, his hero had read) which was awarded to W. L. Gribbon — *honoris causa'* (as an honour for school work) by Boxgrove School in 1891.

Left to Right: Walter Harold Gribbon (Mundy's brother), a cousin Madge Gribbon, and Agnes Margaret "Daisy" Gribbon (Mundy's sister). This picture was taken while Mundy was at Rugby School.
(Courtesy of Maj-Gen. Nigel St. G. Gribbon)

The Times of June 14, 1893, announced a list of boys who had been selected to scholarships at Rugby School. Near the bottom of the list appears the name "Gribbon (Mr. Pridden's Boxgrove)." Willie had sat for the scholarship in the summer of 1893 and came, according to the headmaster's list, sixteenth out of fifty-one candidates. Only twelve scholarships were to be awarded but Willie was considered to be very promising and allowed a special "exhibition," a closed award given either in respect of the recommendation of his preparatory school or because of his father's occupation.

At the beginning of the Winter Terms in September, 1893, Willie went to Rugby School. Rugby is one of England's oldest Public Schools, founded in 1567 by Lawrence Sheriff and made universally famous in Thomas Hughes' novel *Tom Brown's Schooldays.* It is also famous because of the exploit of one of its scholars, William Webb Ellis "who, with a fine disregard for the rules of football as played in his time, first took the ball in his arms and ran with it thus originating the distinctive feature of the Rugby game, A.D. 1825." Among the pupils who afterwards became famous literary personalities were Lewis Carroll, Mathew Arnold, Rupert Brooke, Wyndham Lewis, W. S. Landor and "Nimrod" (Jack Russell).

Willie actually started at the same time as a new headmaster. John Percival, a northern Englishman of decided opinions, had gone to Rugby in 1887 and took over the headship in 1893. Willie had at least one sympathetic memory of Dr. Percival for he recalled, speaking of his timidity and his attempts to disguise it by agressiveness: "At school I fought unnecessary fights because I was afraid to fight them; it was the headmaster of Rugby who skillfully diagnosed that state of mind and walked me out of it."[19]

Willie was placed in the bottom form of the Upper School, which was a very good position for his age. This was in Donkin House. A. E. Donkin, the housemaster, was a master whose name has joined the ranks of the well remembered at Rugby. He was an Etonian who studied mathematics (obtaining a first) at University College, Oxford. Before arriving at Rugby in 1875 he had been a Fellow of Exeter College, a Tutor at Keble and Master at Magdelen College School. He was to resign from Rugby in 1920.

During the Winter Term of 1893 and the Spring Term of 1894 (there were only two terms a year at the Rugby of those days) Willie's academic career seems to have progressed satisfactorily. His name appears in capital letters on the school registers indicating his position as "a scholar." But from the Winter Term of 1894 Willie's scholastic ability seems to have disintegrated into disaster. He lost his "scholarship" status and was hard pressed to keep up with his contemporaries. From the Lower Fifth he was dropped to the form below, called the Upper Middles. His lack of academic status was not even compensated by an interest in sporting activities and throughout his time at Rugby he is not on record as participating in any sporting activities in which the school prided itself.

The total disintegration of his scholastic career, and perhaps the disintegration of part of his character, came in 1895. On Friday, April 19, his father — Walter Galt Gribbon — died of a brain haemorrhage at the age of forty-nine. The official death certificate was made out by Dr. Kane who recorded "diabetes/apoplexy." Diabetes was to run in the Gribbon family causing the death of Daisy Gribbon and eventually of Willie himself. Walter Galt Gribbon had been auditing the books of the English Church Union, in their offices at 35 Wellington Street, WC2, when he had collapsed and died. According to *The Church Review* "Mr. Gribbon was apparently quite well, and occupied with his work with one of the clerks, when before medical assistance could be procured, he expired." According to the *Kingston & Surbiton News* "The funeral took place on Monday, at St. Luke's Church amid many manifestations of sympathy and respect. There was a very large attendance." On Tuesday following the funeral the same newspaper reported that a special meeting was held at St. Luke's Boys' School with Reverend G. I. Swinnerton in the chair, when Walter Galt Gribbon's fellow churchwarden, a Mr. Crowther, described his late colleague "as a man who feared God, honoured the Queen and (was) a good husband and father. Mr. Gribbon had done yeoman service in the parish. In him St. Luke's parish had lost a true friend." He moved:

> That the parishioners of St. Luke's in vestry assembled, desire to take this first opportunity of offering to Mrs. Gribbon and her children their sincere condolence in the afflicting dispensation of Providence with which Mrs. Gribbon and her children have been visited, by the death of Mr. Gribbon, the vicar's warden, and to assure them of their heartfelt participation in the general feeling of sympathy with her and her children under this grievous affliction.

The next evening, Wednesday, the Primrose League met and local Conservative councillor, Colonel Keays, also paid tribute.

The death of his father seems to have unsettled Willie, not only in his school career, but in his whole personality. Within a year of his father's death he began to display his total rebelliousness to his family and society, and embark upon a

A. E. Donkin, Mundy's housemaster at Rugby School, with the pupils of Donkin House, Upper School, Rugby, in 1895. Talbot Mundy (William Lancaster Gribbon) is in the back row, third from the left.
(Courtesy of Rugby School)

career as a wastrel, confidence trickster, drunk and womaniser, so that the well-known travel and adventure writer, Major W. Robert Foran, who knew Willie well for four years in British East Africa, could write: "He was a most barefaced liar and utterly untrustworthy." In later years, Willie never spoke much about his father (nor, indeed, of his family). In fact, he later claimed that he was really the son of the 20th Earl of Shrewsbury. However, he did pay his father the compliment of adopting the name "Walter Galt" as one of his early writing pseudonyms.

During the Winter Term of 1895 Willie did manage to struggle back into the Fifth Form. His contemporaries, such as William Temple, who later became Archbishop of Canterbury, had long passed him by. What must have rankled to young Willie was the fact that his younger brother, Harold, who had followed him through Boxgrove School and entered Rugby in the Winter Term of 1894, was now in the same form as he was.

In December, 1895, Willie was sixteen years and eight months old and still in the Fifth Form. There was a custom at Rugby that if a boy was still in the Fifth Form after his sixteenth birthday he was "superannuated," that is asked to leave. Perhaps due to the death of his father, Dr. Percival and A. E. Donkin, had allowed Willie to remain at Rugby for eight months after this birthday, perhaps hoping that the boy could pull himself together. Willie left Rugby at Christmas, 1895. He always remained bitter about his school life and, in 1931, he wrote to his brother:

> No, I don't have any sympathetic thoughts of Rugby, or of
> Pridden's either. Both places, in my day, were prisons run
> by sadists and inhabited by . . . well, I was one of 'em. It took
> me twenty-five years to begin to shake off what was in me
> when I went there, and was rubbed in by the course they put
> us through. I might have done worse somewhere else, but I
> doubt it. Luckily, I have no child — never had one — not
> even a bastard. Fortune, which equipped me with a marvel-
> lous capacity for trouble, spared me that one horrible re-
> sponsibility. I know I never could screw up the moral cour-
> age to neglect him (or her) as my reason, experience,
> generous impulse and more-or-less modesty argue I should.
> I would certainly try to instruct and "educate." Equally
> certain I would impose on the child a definite percentage
> of my own ideas, not one of which is worth a damn, although

most of them are quite as good as those of other people. Hell
. . . we don't know what it is to live and let live. All of us
appear to have forgotten (if we ever knew it!) that we are
here to learn how to amuse ourselves.[21]

Willie returned home in disgrace. He had been asked to leave school
because he was not displaying sufficient academic ability to remain there. He
had no scholastic qualifications nor the means to enter university. His family
agreed he had charm, personality and was strikingly handsome. But what career
could he embark on? His father's strong support of the Anglican Church may
have been an influencing factor for his mother to decide he should study for
the Anglican priesthood. Walter Galt's friend, the local vicar, Reverend Swinnerton, may have persuaded Mrs. Gribbon that this would be the best course.
In filling out his publisher's publicity questionnaire, Willie wrote against a
heading "The vocation I was advised to follow" — "the Church — the sure haven
for incompetence, but the world was saved in time."[22] In his "Autobiography"
in *Adventure* he recorded:

> My people destined me for the church or the law, I forget
> which, but I know they gave me the choice of two evils and
> that I chose a third that they never even dreamed of. They
> cut off supplies to enforce obedience, and I went without
> supplies — to Germany.[23]

From December, 1895, until the year 1901, Willie Gribbon has, so far, been
successful in hiding his tracks — apart from one or two brief glimpses. His later
accounts of his life from this date until 1911 were so fictionalized as to almost
draw a thick veil over his past. From 1901 onwards, however, diligent research
has revealed most of his astounding story and it is hoped that perhaps the years
1895-1901 may be similarly revealed at a later date. On leaving Rugby School,
family tradition recalls that young Willie was engaged for a brief time on a
newspaper which had offices in Red Lion Square, London and then the newspaper folded within a matter of weeks. There was a confrontation with his mother
about his future career and young Willie ran away.

Willie says his method of choosing a destination was to stick a pin into a
map.

> My pricker landed on a place called Quedlinburg in the
> Harz Mountains, and I arrived there a couple of days later
> with an English five-shilling piece in my pocket, a fox-terrier
> dog on a leash, and a portmanteauful of clothes somewhere
> on the line behind me. I have often wondered who got the
> portmanteau.[24]

Quedlinburg was a medium sized town in north Germany, just to the south of Hanover and standing on the River Bode. In 1932, while driving through Germany with his fifth wife, Dawn, Willie was to stop in Quedlinburg to recall memories of his rebellious youth. One can therefore be fairly certain that Willie's stories of his flight to Germany were founded in fact.

Unable to speak German, young Willie managed to make friends with the driver of a traction engine who worked for a circus, towing vans. The man needed an assistant and Willie persuaded him that he could drive the engine. Willie at this time looked far older than he actually was. He was a handsome, fair haired youth, already well over six feet in height. With the driver's influence, the circus proprietor employed Willie at ten marks a week as assistant driver. The driver added another eight marks a week for Willie to do all the work and allow him to get drunk (his favourite occupation) and take any blame if things went wrong.

> It turned out to be a good job, and I liked it, and I found out
> all there was to know about that traction engine in a very
> short time. We had a steam roundabout and swings and box-
> ing booths, and some wild animals in cases along with the
> circus; in fact, it was almost a travelling fair.

But Willie and his driver friend quarrelled when, in a drunken mood, the man killed his fox-terrier. Willie quit his job and made his way back to Qued-linburg. He succeeded in picking up another job but apart from recalling it was "a good job" and that "I made good, but didn't like it" Willie recounted nothing about his next occupation. He hinted that it was something to do with agriculture and later biographical notices recorded that "he spent a year in Germany, studying agriculture" and one article stated that he was studying at a German University. Willie spent the whole of 1896 in Germany but he was not able to keep himself as independently as he later claimed. He even admitted, when asked about his first attempt at writing, that it was "home to my mother for money. Best fiction I ever did."[25]

Willie's family persuaded him to return to England. Willie put a different slant on things. "A man back in England happened to hear that I had made good and hired me at a salary that was absolutely enormous for a boy of seventeen...."[26] The man, however, was Willie's uncle, William Sharpe of Bardney, and Willie's cousin, Mrs. May Nicholson, recalls that Willie arrived to stay with them, after his return from Germany, and announced he wanted to go in for farming and estate management and asked whether his uncle could help him. His uncle agreed and allowed Willie to help on the estate in return for his board and lodging and a small salary. Willie's version is:

> My new employer had a pecularity that is not at all uncommon among men of his type in England; he loved buying expensive hunters, but he had not always the nerve to ride them; so quite a large part of my duties consisted in riding his hunters for him three days a week or so during the season. Besides being splendid sport and keeping me in excellent condition, the experience gave me a knowledge of horsemanship and woodcraft that has been invaluable since.[27]

In contradiction to this, ten years after this article appeared, Willie confessed "I have never become a good horseman" and that horses always made him feel nervous. This is confirmed by Richard Ames, his stepson and son of his fourth wife (1923-31), who says that his erstwhile stepfather was a terrible horseman.[28]

> I piled up money, though, because I hadn't a chance to spend it. As a matter of fact I piled up too much money and that, and the fact that I was barely twenty-one and that my job had grown monotonous, got me going with a map of the world and the sticker again.[29]

It is now we enter a very confusing period in Willie's life — the exact date he left Bardney to go to India. In 1901 Willie was definitely in Bombay and described as being "a merchant." Mrs. May Nicholson recalls quite distinctly that Willie spent his twenty-first birthday, April 23, 1900, at Bardney, and a local Bardney newspaper of June 14, 1900, places him still on the Sharpe's estate on June 7 helping to organise a celebration in honour of the raising of the British flag in Pretoria.

In most of his reminiscences, Willie maintained that he went to India in 1900 (which would seem a fairly accurate date) but, having spent time organising famine relief in Baroda, being a newspaper correspondent on the North West Frontier, trekking across India into the forbidden territory of Tibet and travelling to China, Singapore, the Straits Settlements and sailing to the Persian Gulf, Willie also maintained that he had enlisted in a volunteer cavalry unit which fought at Colseno and at Ladysmith. He said he carried despatches at Colseno and was wounded at Ladysmith and invalided out of the army. Historically, this is impossible, because Colenso was fought in December, 1899, and Ladysmith was relieved in February, 1900. Further, in another article in *Adventure*, Willie claimed that he had served in the British Army for six years! Only the *Publishers Weekly* seemed to have caught the discrepancies between the dates he went to India and the date of the Boer War and suggested that he was eighteen when he went to India[30], thus adding feasibility to the story that he went to India in 1897 and joined up in 1899.

However, many of the stories which Willie subsequently told about his adventures are demonstrably false. He was never in the army nor did he see action in the Boer War. Other tales, such as his meeting with Rudyard Kipling in Bright, are quite feasible (and it is true that Kipling did correspond with him) but these have yet to be corroborated. Some tales may never be confirmed, such as his claim that he returned to India in 1901 as a correspondent for the *Daily Mail* and covered disturbances on the North West Frontier. No despatches carrying his name appeared in the *Mail* at this time but then by-lined articles were only accorded to well known correspondents such as Edgar Wallace.

Therefore, for the purposes of this particular essay, I propose to recount only the facts that can be verified at this particular time. It seems that Willie, having spent some time on William Sharpe's estate at Bardney, left for India in the autumn of 1900. According to Mrs. May Nicholson: "We never saw him after that year. He went off on his travels and finally to America. My sister saw him once in New York and reported that he had not changed very much." It could well be that Willie went to Baroda to help with famine relief as he claimed, for India was certainly struck with famine and plague in 1900, but what is verifiable is that William Lancaster Gribbon was in Bombay in 1901, not as a governmental official nor as a newspaper correspondent, but as a merchant.

From 1901 we can follow Willie's strange career with complete accuracy.

In Bombay Willie met Kathleen Steele, the fourth and youngest daughter of William Johnstone Steele, from Edinburgh, Scotland, who was a director of the London branch of the Royal Bank of New Zealand. Kathleen was a year younger than Willie. They fell in love and became engaged.

In 1902 Willie followed Kathleen home to London and later that year he helped to form a merchant company called Walton & Co., who had offices at 35 Lamb's Conduit Street, in London's West End. Willie appears as senior director of the firm and it seems a fairly reasonable speculation that he financed his business enterprise with a considerable sum of money which he inherited from his father's estate on his 21st birthday in 1900. But his inheritance did not last long. The Gribbon family are all agreed that he inherited "quite a large sum of money" from his father's estate and that "he led a very gay life in London and spent practically every penny of his allowance." Willie's own tales of how he spent his inheritance vary but a favourite tale seems to be that he left it in the safekeeping of a friend in India while he went off to fight in the Boer War.

On January 31, 1903, Willie, then aged twenty-three years, married Kathleen Steele at the Anglican church of St. John the Evangelist, Westminster. The officiating priest was his father's old friend, Reverend George Isaac Swinnerton of St. Luke's, Kingston Hill. *The Times* carried a brief notice of the wedding and Willie was described as "a merchant" living at Elmscroft, Cranes Park, Surbiton, which was, in fact, his mother's address. Kathleen was described as "a spinster" living at 55 Westminster Mansions, Great Smith Street, London SW1. Her father was now dead and her mother was listed as living in Bedfordshire. Willie's own mother signed as a witness and the best-man was named as Richard Belt.

According to Willie's brother: "From about 1903 onwards I did not see my brother for many years. He had an adventurous career before settling down as a successful author under the name of Talbot Mundy."[31]

Willie had, in fact, promised Kathleen a honeymoon which involved sailing around the world, starting out via the Cape of Good Hope. Arrangements had been made but at the last minute Willie claimed that business affairs would detain him in England and that Kathleen should start alone for South Africa, where her brother Graham Steele was living. Willie would join her there within a few weeks. Kathleen sailed from Southampton on the *SS Gascon* (of the Union Castle Line) on February 28. With her she took, as a companion, a friend — Miss Cobb.[32]

What Willie had not informed Kathleen was that he was in grave financial trouble, deeply in debt and under suspicion for shady transactions in stocks and shares. In fact, Erskine Oxenford & Co., stock and share brokers, were already contemplating action against him. They filed a petition against Willie in the Court of Bankruptcy on April 25 stating he was trading under the name of Walton & Co. but in May, when a receiving order was made on May 29, the name of the firm was deleted. Apparently Willie had sold his shares to his partners and the firm remained in business until 1905. Probably with the proceeds of this transaction Willie sailed on the *RMS Norman* (of the Union Castle Line) on March 28, 1903,[33] from Southampton. He left just before the legal papers were served on him and the public examination was held on July 23 in his absence. Adjudication was made on July 25 and he was officially pronounced as a bankrupt. A notice to that effect appeared in *The Times* of August 1.

William Lancaster Gribbon arrived in Cape Town on April 14 where he joined Kathleen and her friend Miss Cobb who had arrived on March 24. Willie rented a house in Cape Town called "Glengariff" where Kathleen's brother, Graham Steele, visited them and introduced Willie to local businessmen. Willie started to borrow money for a business venture but, apparently, with no prospect of paying anyone back. The storm was about to burst and Willie told his wife he had got into financial difficulties. He suggested that Kathleen and Miss Cobb return to England and he would follow them when he had sorted matters out. On July 8, 1903, Kathleen and Miss Cobb sailed from Cape Town on the *RMS Walmer Castle* (which reached London on August 1). She was never to see Willie again.

Within a few days the police in Cape Town had issued a warrant for the arrest of William Lancaster Gribbon for debt.[34] But Willie had disappeared. Later that year, Kathleen Gribbon received a letter from Willie dated October 31 and addressed from Chai Chai, on the Limpopo River, in Portuguese East Africa, telling her that he was using the name Thomas Hartley. He appears to have borrowed the name from a former Rugby School classmate named Thomson Hartley.

It is speculation as to where Willie went from July until October. Certainly he could not have remained in Cape Town. According to Willie's own tales of his adventures, when he left Cape Town having been wounded in the Boer War, he sailed on a ship to Sydney, Australia, with an Englishman named Charlie. From Sydney he tramped all the way to Brisbane, becoming tramps or "sundowners." On reaching Brisbane, Willie says they took a job stoking in a small steamer and reached Hobart in Tasmania. Charlie elected to stay in Hobart while Willie took a job on a three-masted barque heading for Portuguese East Africa. When the ship put in at Lorenco Marques, the entire crew (including himself) "jumped ship" because of bad conditions.[35] Can we believe this part of his story? It is certainly true that Willie disappeared from Cape Town and re-appeared in Chai Chai.

> I got so low with fever, and so absolutely busted, that I was glad to accept the hospitality of a Chinese laundryman; he put me between clean sheets and fed me back to health again. Then he told me where to go and get a job! I landed the job at the first try, and it was a good one, too, if you reckon without the climate. . . . I had to run a big estate up the Limpopo River, and while doing it I am glad to say that I was able to help my friend the Chinaman.[36]

Willie confirms that this estate was at Chai Chai from where Kathleen received her letter.

Kathleen Gribbon immediately wrote to Willie but the letter was returned through the Dead Letter Office.[37] Willie says he had another bout of fever which hit him so badly that he gave up his job and moved northward to seek a more favourable climate.

> The British East African Government had just finished the railway to the Lake (Victoria), and the country was being boomed like wild fire, so I decided to go there and took the very first steamer with the idea of getting well again on the way up.[38]

On January 27, 1904, the steamer *Bundesrath* of the Deutsche Ost-Afrika Linie, arrived at Lourenco Marques from Port Natal. Thomas Hartley joined the passengers and the ship reached Zanzibar on February 5. The *Bundesrath* was used by Willie as the ship in which his heroes arrive at Zanzibar when he came to write *The Ivory Trail*. Willie, or rather, Tom Hartley, was in Mombasa on February 10, a fact reported in the *African Standard* of February 13.

According to Willie, on arrival in British East Africa, he hired a native called Kazi Moto as a personal servant and set out to earn his living as a hunter. He later told journalist Archie Kilpatrick that he organised a group of natives to hunt elephants for their ivory.

The local authorities ruled his expedition to be poaching and issued a warrant for his arrest. On his hunting he found a herd of about 4,000 cattle bearing the brand of a government official who, under the law, was entitled to own but two animals.

He undertook to drive the cattle into German East Africa but the official sent a company of native warriors to stop him and there was a battle. The adventurer was wounded by a spear in his leg, and while he was ill heard the natives digging a grave for him. That brought him out of it in a hurry.[39]

Another version appeared in Willie's autobiographical article in *Adventure:*

I didn't get rich at the game (hunting) but I made enough to pay my men and I got hold of a good mob of cattle which I drove over the border into German territory. A marauding band of Masai tackled me not far from Shirati and drove off the whole lot. Naturally I resented it and, in the process of doing so, I received a spear-wound in my right leg. Kazi Moto killed my assailant with the butt end of a gun . . .

With the Masai having taken his cattle, "my only visible wealth," Willie says he was broke and suffering from illness as a result of wound infection. He reached Muanza where he fell prey to a severe attack of Blackwater fever. At one point the local doctor told Kazi Moto, as Willie lay on his sick bed, that he would be dead by afternoon and it would be best to dig a grave. "I hated the man so, and was utterly disgusted with his treatment of me, that I made up my mind to disappoint him, and from that minute I began to get better."

Hunting ivory not only provided Willie with background for his adventure stories but also for articles such as "Elephant Hunting for a Living" which he wrote under his pseudonym of Walter Galt and "Random Reminiscences of African Big Game" under Talbot Mundy.[40]

On October 15, 1904, William Robert Foran was appointed Assistant District Superintendent of the British East African Police and sent to Port Florence, also known as Kisumu, the chief port on Lake Victoria and terminus of the railway. He was to be police chief there with a European sergeant, 75 askaris and 25 Indian policemen. He recalled:

At my introduction to Kisumu it was no more than a frontier town of mushroom growth, brought into being by the railway terminus and shipbuilding yards — much in the same way as Nairobi. The railway station was a corrugated iron building similar to all others, and situated close to the jetty and Indian bazaar, while, on the hill overlooking the town and lake, were the Government offices, residence of the officials, the jail and police barracks — not forgetting the post office.

The only sources of social gaiety and recreation available were the tennis courts near the office of the Provincial Commissioner and the Nyanza Club. The Railway Institute had a sports ground where cricket matches were played on occasions. It was far too hot for football (Rugby or Association) or even hockey, the ground being terribly hard for those games.

There were no roads — only rough tracks. One led from the railway station to the crest of the hill; and another started at the same point and, after traversing the Indian bazaar, also led by a circumtous route to the hill. Both roads ended just beyond the tennis courts. A start was being made, however, to improve the existing thoroughfares and construct new ones.

Not more than twenty Europeans lived in Kisumu and seldom were there at the same time. White women had not yet appeared in the township.

In short, Foran said "Kisumu was no health resort in those pioneer days." The temperature seldom fell below 100 degrees (F).[41]

Writing to *Adventure's* editor, A. S. Hoffman, in later[25] years, Foran recalled of Talbot Mundy: "I first met him at Kisumu in 1904, when he had been posing as Sir Rupert Harvey, Baronet, and had stung a lot of business firms! I arrested him on a warrant from the High Court and he was given six months with hard labour."[42] There was no such person in Debrett's as Sir Rupert Harvey but there was a Sir Robert Grenville Harvey (Baronet) who arrived at Mombasa on November 13, 1904, to give evidence against the man making free with his name.

On his release, Willie returned to the name Thomas Hartley and, being a persuasive and personable young man, he persuaded Foran that he repented his past mistakes. According to Foran; "I got him a job as the first Town Clerk of Kisumu and he behaved well for a time. . . ." Indeed, on December 3, 1905, Willie was able to write to his wife Kathleen that he was now passing as Thomas Hartley at Kisumu and was in Government service as town clerk.

Kathleen was, naturally, very unhappy about the situation and corresponded with Willie on the matter. On May 17, 1907, Willie finally replied:

> Dear Kathleen — It seems rather absurd that you should write and ask me after all this time whether I have been faithful to you or not. You can probably answer the question yourself without asking me. However, judging by the tenor of your letter, I should say you are contemplating divorce, and, as I honestly think that this would be the best course you could pursue, it seems unfair that I should withhold any information that might be of assistance to you, especially as I don't suppose I shall ever see you again. There is no good to be gained by dragging in any third party, but it will serve your purpose if I admit that I have been unfaithful to you. I have been so for the last three years. I advise you to divorce me at once, and wish you luck. We could never have got on together anyhow. — Your husband, W. L. Gribbon.[43]

To say he had been unfaithful was merely an understatement for in Kisumu Willie's numerous affairs with native women had become so notorious that he was widely known by an uncomplimentary Swahili nickname — *Makundu Viazi*, which, in its politest and un-literal form, meant "white arse."[44] But, apart from his affairs with native women, Willie was having an affair with Inez Broom Craven, the wife of the Hon. Rupert Craven, which was eventually to lead to his dismissal from his job as town clerk.

The Cravens had arrived in British East Africa early in 1906. W. R. Foran recalled:

> I remember well the joyous arrival of a cheery quartette of settlers — the Hon. Charles and the Hon. Rupert Craven, with their respective wives; Jackie Lethbidge; and Jim Elkington, his wife and small daughter. Charles Craven was a former subaltern in the Grenadier Guards, a noted boxer in Army circles and several times won the officers' heavyweight championships at Aldershot. His brother Rupert was

an ex-lieutenant in the Royal Navy. Jackie Lethbidge had been a captain in the Gunners, returning after the Boer War. The Cravens eventually became partners in ivory hunting in the Lado Enclave region of the Belgian Congo, where Charles died of Blackwater fever towards the end of 1909 and was buried at Koba (on the British side of the Nile). His death was mourned by all.

Inez Craven was a noted English beauty. She had been born Inez Harriette Elena Broom on February 26, 1873, the daughter of George Broom, a noted and respected member of the Reform Club and Marlborough Club. Inez had been born near Wokingham. She achieved a reputation for her unusual beauty, a reputation as a daring cross-country rider and a notoriety for leading a London bachelor girl existence — living alone in London — smoking and drinking, all of which scandalised Victorian English society at the time. In 1899 her notoriety increased when she was named in a divorce case in which Kathleen Chandos-Pole sued for divorce from her husband Samuel Chandos-Pole on the grounds of cruelty and his adultery with Inez.

Inez had married the Hon. Rupert Cecil Craven OBE, the second son of the 3rd Earl of Craven, on April 9, 1898. This was after the alleged adultery with Chandos-Pole which was supposed to have happened in 1896. Rupert Craven had been an officer in the Royal Navy but was now training to be an engineer. He kicked-off the publicity scandal by assaulting the solicitor's clerk who served the papers on his wife and then accused Sir George Lewis (the solicitor appearing for Mrs. Chandos-Pole) of "buying evidence." Craven was fined for assault a few weeks prior to the trial. The first jury could not agree on Inez' involvement and a second trial was held and the case against Inez was finally dismissed. She played the *femme fatale* role well, and became a talking point not only of Edwardian England but also of America as well.

According to Foran:

(Mundy) "behaved well for a time but later got tied-up with the Hon. Mrs. Rupert Craven, formerly Inez Broom, and a noted lady rider in Britain. She was a bad lot and drank like a fish." This is confirmed by the letters Rupert Craven sent to his mother. Early in 1908 the Kisii tribe in the Kisumu area rose up in rebellion and Foran formed part of the punitive expedition to quell the tribesmen. "I was away on the Kisii Expedition early in 1908 and on my return found they (Mundy and Inez Craven) had the cheek to be living together in my official house. I promptly turned them out. Rupert Craven then arrived, there was a terrific row on the veranda of my house, and he started a divorce and got it. Mundy lost his job as Town Clerk but was given another on an island in the Victoria Lake, where they lived together as man and wife."

Craven was bitter. He wrote to his mother:

> I found she had bolted with this man who had come out especially for the purpose. Well, I'm not going to act the jealous husband for a worthless jade and so I will let them just stew in, say, their own grease. The letters alone would have got me my freedom but this act is the climax.
>
> You know what I have been through in the last ten years; tho' to give her her due I believe she has, up to now, been faithful. But I practically renounced everything to marry and this is the result. I cannot say I had any affection left but was willing to try and do my best but I am no longer a youngster and am not inclined to be Quixotic.
>
> The divorce will, I am given to understand, be undefended and I must get hold of the money for the fees somehow. I don't think it will cost more than £50 or £75 but at present all the money I had as my share of the ivory is spent as I gave it to her. But divorce her I will now and thank heaven to be free. The worst punishment I could wish for the man Hartley is to be saddled with her. Her drinking habits he will quickly discover and indeed I believe that the lapse is now caused by my having no spirits on the journey. . . . I have always been thankful I have no children.[45]

Rupert Craven received his divorce in the District Registry of the High Court of the East African Protectorate at Kisumu and the decree absolute was granted on November 7, 1908. He named Thomas Hartley as corespondent.

In the meantime, Willie's career as Thomas Hartley was running short of time. His wife Kathleen had instituted divorce proceedings on December 3, 1907 in London and Mr. Justice Bargrave Deane granted permission for a special commission to be held in Nairobi to examine native witnesses as to Willie's adultery and to allow Kathleen's brother, Graham, who was on a journey from New Zealand and passing through Nairobi, to formally identify Thomas Hartley as William Lancaster Gribbon.

B. G. Allen, the commissioner, sitting at Nairobi in January, heard evidence that William Lancaster Gribbon was not only known as Thomas Hartley but *Lord* Hartley as well. Graham Steele also told the commission that a warrant for Willie's arrest was still current in Cape Town.

Evidence was then given about Willie's affairs and it was revealed that Willie had "habitually committed adultery" with various native women but, in particular, Fatuma, the daughter of Urandet of the Nandi tribe; Chesui, daughter of Matia Kingi of the Kamasia tribe; and with Habiba, daughter of Hassan of the Waganda tribe. All three women gave evidence to the hearing. Evidence was then given that Willie "had been cited as corespondent in the name of Thomas Hartley in divorce proceedings in the High Court of the East African Protectorate sitting in Kisumu by the Hon. Rupert Cecil Craven against his wife Inez Craven née Broom. . . ."

On May 4, in London, Mr. Justice Bargrave Deane heard the rest of the evidence and found the case proved. He granted Kathleen a decree absolute to come into effect on November 9, 1908.

The case caused a scandal in London with the *News of the World* headlining it as "MAKUNDU VIAZI — Town Clerk's Intrigues with Tribeswomen — Corespondent in Society Suit Now Divorced"[46] and even the sedate *Times'* report was followed up by a correspondence in the letters' column.[47]

For a while, it seems, Thomas Hartley and Inez Craven lived on the island in Lake Victoria. Then, in June, 1908, W. R. Foran recalls: "Before I went on leave they arrived back in Kisumu destitute. I arrested both under the Distressed British Subjects' Act, they were given six months in the prison at Mombasa and, on completion of this, shipped off to India on a deportation order." The penal code operating in British East Africa at that time was the British India Penal Code whereby vagrants and undesirables would be picked up and would serve six months at the Fort, Mombasa, which earnt them their passage to Bombay, to which all undesirables were shipped.

Major W. R. Foran left British East Africa in July, 1908, and did not return until 1909. He assumed that Willie and Inez were deported in the usual fashion and did not see Willie again until 1913 when, having become a well-known travel and adventure writer himself, he was in the offices of *Adventure* magazine talking with A. S. Hoffman, the editor, who introduced him to his "star" contributor — Talbot Mundy. Later Foran wrote to Hoffman: "(It) must have been a shock for him, but I hid the fact that he was well known to me. Perhaps I should have told you his past record and warned you about him, but I hate to rub it in after a man has paid the price of his misdeeds and, also, we were both contributing to *Adventure*."

But *had* Willie and Inez been deported in November, 1908, having served their six months prison sentence?

The *East Africa Standard* of November 21 recorded that during the preceeding week a T. C. Miller Mundy of Nairobi had registered at the Africa Hotel, Mombasa. On November 19 Talbot Chetwynd Miller Mundy (giving his correct age of 29 years) and Inez Craven (who gave her age as 31 years) were married at the Mombasa Registry Office. Mundy described himself as a "gentleman" and gave his father's name as the Earl of Shrewsbury and Waterford.

William Lancaster Gribbon had chosen his final pseudonym and one which he was to live with for the rest of his life. In choosing his previous name of Thomas Hartley he had recalled his Rugby School classmate's name of Thomson Hartley. How, then, did he choose the name of Talbot Chetwynd Miller Mundy? He had stated on his marriage certificate to Inez Craven that the Earl of Shrewsbury was his father and, in later years, W. R. Foran fully believed this and wrote (in his letter to Hoffman): "that was his name, and he was an illegitimate son of the Earl of Shrewsbury and Mrs. Mundy, wife of a Colonel Mundy."

Willie certainly chose the name carefully, because it was a name with an authentic background. He had chosen for his "father" the 20th Earl of Shrewsbury, who was Premier Earl of England, Hereditary Great Seneschal (Lord High Steward) of Ireland, and Great Steward of the Borough of Stafford; a peer who held a very prominent position in English society. In addition, the 20th Earl of Shrewsbury had had an affair with Ellen Mary Miller Mundy, the wife of Alfred Edward Miller Mundy of Shipley Hall, Derby. In 1881, a scandal had been created when Mrs. Miller Mundy ran off with the Earl but they eventually married in 1882 and their son Charles John Alton Chetwynd was born on September 8, that year, conceived out of wedlock but born in it. Willie knew enough about the family to choose his names well.

The name Talbot he took from the fact that among the titles of the Earl of Shrewsbury (who also held the title of Earl of Waterford — as Willie currently stated on his marriage certificate) were the titles Baron *Talbot* of Hensal (created in 1733) and Earl *Talbot* in Hensal (created in 1784). The name *Chetwynd* is a family name of the Shrewsburies and the name *Miller Mundy* was, of course, the name of the 20th Earl's wife. Willie even knew enough to write Miller Mundy without a hyphen, one of the few old English double-barrelled names that is so written.

Willie must, therefore, have had access to a very up-to-date Debbrett's Peerage, or had met one or other of the families involved to acquire these intimate details. Major P. Miller Mundy, the grandson of Alfred Edward (whose wife ran away with the 20th Earl) still lives in London and ironically had read Talbot Mundy's books as a young man. He could recall no family link with Willie Gribbon nor that any of the family were ever in any part of the world at the same time as Willie.

A curious light on Willie's second marriage is that on November 26, 1908, Inez wrote from Mombasa to Lady Craven (in order to forward on a bill which, she claimed, Rupert Craven should have paid). In this letter she signs herself "Inez Craven," crosses it out, and re-signs "Inez Miller Mundy." She then created confusion about her marriage by stating:

> The Church considers that my previous marriage to a Protestant can be made null and void and have written to Rome, in the meantime we have received the Apostelic Benediction.

But in no way was there any Catholic involvement in the marriage. In an interview given on October 3, 1909, Inez showed she could be the equal of Willie for a handy tale:

> During a hunting trip which she and her husband (Craven) took she made the acquaintance of Mundy, one of whose ancestors had married into the Earl of Shrewsbury's family. He had knocked about in the navy, the army, and the civil service as many adventurous young Englishmen do. At the time Mrs. Craven and her husband first met him, on their African hunting trip, he was District Commissioner of Port Florence, East Africa.
>
> After Mrs. Craven got her divorce she went back to East Africa, according to her story yesterday, and married Mundy ten months ago. Mundy, at that time, had either lost or in some way got out of, his small civil service place.[48]

It has, so far, been difficult to ascertain whether Willie and Inez were deported to India as W. R. Foran thought. However, in early 1909, they were back in London as Mr. and Mrs. T. C. Miller Mundy. According to Inez, in her interview, they had gone to London where Willie had tried to get a job on a newspaper. He maintained that "He had done some newspaper work once, having been connected with the London *Mail*."

This was the last time that Willie was to see his mother, Margaret Gribbon. Mrs. Gribbon set out to India in 1913 to visit her second son — Walter Harold Gribbon. While on the journey, on the P&O ship *SS Mantua*, she died of Uraemia, Brights (Kidney) Disease on Sunday, November 2, shortly after the ship left Marseilles and was buried at sea on November 4.

Willie's brother was then a Staff Captain in the King's Own Scottish Borderers in the Ahmednagar Brigade in India. On leaving Rugby he had received a commission in the army. He had last seen Willie in 1903 and was not to see him again until 1933. Willie's brother was eventually to become a Brigadier having served in the First World War in the Middle East as an Intelligence Officer, fluent in Turkish, and ending the war as a Brevet Lieutenant-Colonel. In 1928 he was appointed Brigadier commanding the Canal Brigade in Egypt. As well as being a Companion of the Order of St. Michael and St. George, a Commander of the British Empire, he was also awarded the Star of Rumania, the White Eagle VI Class (Serbia), the Legion of Honour (France) and the Order of St. Anne (Russia). His career remarkably resembled many of Willie's heroes and one cannot help wondering whether Willie looked with perhaps a little envy at his younger brother's military record. Brigadier W. H. Gribbon died on December 18, 1944, at the age of sixty-three at his home at "Galt," Hythe, Kent.

He seems to have carried on a military tradition in the Gribbon family which went back at least as far as the Napoleonic Wars. A James Gribbon served in the 40th Foot Regiment (afterwards the 2nd Somerset) which fought through the Peninsula Campaign, in Portugal and Spain, and were among the British regiments which Andrew Jackson turned back before New Orleans in the Anglo-American War of 1812. The regiment finally faced Napoleon as part of the Duke of Wellington's "thin red line" at Waterloo in 1815. Later, an uncle of Willie's, G. C. Gribbon, became Brigade-Surgeon of the King's Own Scottish Borders. Walter Harold Gribbon's eldest son, Nigel St. George Gribbon, born on February 6, 1917, also took up this tradition and, after an education at Rugby and Sandhurst, was also commissioned into the King's Own. He went on to become a Major-General before his retirement in 1972.

Willie's sister, Daisy, had married the 29-year-old headmaster of a local preparatory school named Ernest William Webb on September 10, 1904. She had three children, two girls and a boy, but the marriage started to break up. Early in 1914 she ran away with a local doctor named Walker. They finally married and she had a son named Bruce. Daisy died in September, 1939, significantly from complications produced by diabetes — the same condition as Walter Galt Gribbon died from — and the same condition that led to Willie's own death in 1940. On August 5, 1939, he wrote to his brother:

> I feel very sorry for Daisy. Diabetes can be depressing beyond the imagination of anyone who has not suffered from it. One of its worst symptoms is that it saps that inner energy with which it is sometimes possible to meet and to overcome the slings and arrows that fate hurls against us. It sets up a vicious circle. the disease undermines the will, and the weakening will will increase the disease. I suppose she is having injections of insulin? The doctors some times overdo that. Too little sugar in the blood is even worse than too much sugar. I have made a note of Daisy's address and will write to her again before long.

But within a few weeks Daisy was dead and exactly a year to the day he wrote the letter, Willie himself had also fallen a victim to the malady.

Willie and Inez did not stay long in England. On September 22, 1909, they sailed from Southampton on the White Star Line, *SS Teutonic* which arrived at New York on September 29. It was a Thursday and the couple had with them $500 in English money which they immediately had changed into American currency. On Thursday evening Willie rented a room in a tenement block at 503 East Fifteenth Street. According to the *New York Times* "it soon became noised around the saloons of the neighbourhood that the green Englishman and his wife had sufficient money to be worth the risk of robbing."[48] The newspaper reported:

> Three men called at the Mundys' tenement rooms on Friday afternoon. Mundy was out at the time. They told Mrs. Mundy they wanted to look at the rooms with a view to renting them and offered to send out and get some beer. They were in and out of the rooms several times during the day and during the evening enticed Mundy out to a saloon apparently for a card game.
>
> One of the men returned a few minutes afterwards and tried to steal Mrs. Mundy's watch. She had an English policeman's whistle and blew it. The whole tenement was aroused and a crowd of nearly 500 collected in the streets.

Talbot Mundy's brother, Walter Harold Gribbon, at his marriage to Edith Margaret Stuart in 1908. Walter Gribbon rose to the rank of Brigadier General, and his military career paralleled that of some of his brother's fictional heroes.

(Courtesy of Maj-Gen. Nigel St. G. Gribbon)

Mundy failed to return from the card game. But shortly after midnight the night watchman of a Nineteenth Street factory found him unconscious and bleeding on the sidewalk. His pockets were empty and he had apparently been blackjacked and robbed.[49]

On Saturday the *New York Times* blazed the story on page one

— THUGS BEAT TALBOT MUNDY —
HUSBAND OF NOTED ENGLISH BEAUTY MAY DIE.

Willie, or Talbot Mundy as he now would be for the rest of his life, had a fractured skull. He was taken to a public ward in Bellevue Hospital. He recovered consciousness, however, late the following day while Inez was in "a dingy First Avenue saloon" (according to the *New York Times)* busy telling the story of her life . . . for the price of a drink.

> "I must have a cigarette and a brandy and soda," she said to the newspaper men who asked her if she would say anything on her vicissitudes.

According to her story, it was she who had divorced Rupert Craven and, she told reporters, "I love him — I love him as deeply as ever."[51]

Willie eventually recovered and a Joseph Cahill, a driver, of 500 West Fifty-Third Street, was arrested by Detective Barry of the East Twenty-Second Street Station for the crime. According to Willie, it was while laying in Bellevue Hospital that he commenced to write his first serious articles. Certainly, a year later Talbot Mundy was finding a ready market for his stories in *Adventure* magazine.

By 1912 his stories were in demand by some very prestigious British magazines such as *Strand, Pall Mall, London Magazine* and the *Grand.* And, in 1914, his first novel, RUNG HO!, had been published both in America and in Britain to a high critical acclaim. William Lancaster Gribbon and Thomas Hartley had vanished and Talbot Mundy had established himself on the road to a lasting fame as one of the highest paid and bestselling writers of adventure fiction of his day. His forty-odd books appeared both in the USA and UK and were translated into nearly a dozen languages. Serialisations, short stories and articles from his pen appeared in a wide variety of magazines from *Adventure* to the *Saturday Evening Post* and from the *Strand* to *Pall Mall.* Critics hailed him as "Kipling's nearest rival" (a comparison he found odious) and compared his literary status with that of Sir Henry Rider Haggard.

Gone completely was Willie the wastrel, confidence trickster, and drunk; gone also was the need to call himself Talbot Chetwynd Miller Mundy. And it was as plain Talbot Mundy that he was granted American citizenship on March 14, 1917.

His last links with his past were severed (at least for the next twenty years) when on June 19, 1912, Inez sued him for divorce (on the grounds of his repeated adultery) before Justice Leonard A. Giegerich at the New York County Court House in the Borough of Manhattan. It was found "that the defendant is guilty of the adultery charged in the complaint." The final decree was made on October 10, 1912. The judge made an order for her to receive "alimony at the rate of Twenty Dollars ($20.00) per week" payable by Mundy. There was also a condition to the divorce.

> . . . and it is further ordered, adjudged and decreed, that it shall be lawful for the plaintiff Inez Miller Mundy to marry again during the lifetime of the defendant Talbot Miller Mundy, in the same manner as if the defendant were dead, *but it shall not be lawful for the defendant Talbot Miller Mundy, to marry any other person until the said plaintiff, Inez Miller Mundy shall be dead. . . .*

It seems a strange and rather unjust judgement. Nevertheless, it did not bother Mundy. Within a few months, in Stamford, Connecticut, on August 21, 1913, Mundy married Harriette Rosemary Strafer, a well known portrait and miniature painter six years his senior. And, although a court in Reno, Nevada, forbade Mundy to divorce and remarry anywhere in the United States in a 1923 judgement,[52] Mundy divorced and married twice more in Mexico.

As for Inez, she returned to calling herself Mrs. Craven and joined the Suffragette Movement in New York, taking part in the protest march in Albany as a prominent member in December, 1912. Her drink problem continued to grow worse and in January, 1913, she was committed to Bellevue suffering from hallucinations.[53] It is interesting that, at this time, she claimed she was a Theosophist because, in 1923, Mundy himself became a member of Madam Katherine Tingley's inner ruling cabinet of the Theosophist Movement at Point Loma, California, and one of its chief protagonists.

From 1911 Talbot Mundy the writer seemed to have little connection with his previous life. It was as if he had stepped abruptly out of nowhere into a new role in life. In fact, one of his favourite quotations in his later life was from Shakespeare's *As You Like It:*

> All the world's a stage
> And all the men and women merely players.
> They have their exits and their entrances
> *And one man in his time plays many parts.*

It can be said that Mundy played four distinct roles in his life: — William Lancaster Gribbon 1879-1903; Thomas Hartley 1904-08; Talbot Chetwynd Miller Mundy 1908-11 and Talbot Mundy 1911-40. And it is, of course, by the role of Talbot Mundy that he is remembered today; a role he played with such consistency and determination that not even those closest to him knew of his life prior to 1911.

To merely say that Mundy was a scoundrel and that he lived a lie from 1911 in order to cover up his past misdeeds would be to simplify matters to the point of distortion. He was a deep, intriguing and complex personality; a man of personal magnetism and great charisma. Moreover, he was a romantic, possessed of a literary skill and imagination given to few writers; a writer who has earned a distinguished place in the Valhalla of literature.

NOTES

1   In 1922 he was receiving $2,500 per month from *Adventure* alone, as well as contributing to numerous other magazines in Britain and to other publications in the U.S.A. In addition there were royalties from his book sales and, in 1923, the first film of one of his novels (HER REPUTATION) was released.

2   Birth certificate (General Registrar of Births, Deaths & Marriages, London) and Baptismal certificate No. 208 & letter from Brigadier W. H. Gribbon to Messrs Bickerton Pratt (solicitors) April 21, 1944.

3   A DICTIONARY OF BRITISH SURNAMES ed. P. H. Reaney (Routledge & Kegan Paul, London, 1958).

4   Undated cutting in family scrapbook.

5   Undated obituary in family scrapbook.

6   Talbot Mundy to brother W. H. Gribbon, July 26, 1937.

7   *Kingston & Surbiton News,* July, 1896.

8   TM to W. H. Gribbon August 1, 1937.

9   TM to W. H. Gribbon August 5, 1939.

10   Now Mrs. May Nicholson in interview with writer April 29, 1977.

11   Undated cutting in family scrapbook.

12   TM to W. H. Gribbon November 20, 1939.

13   Random Reminiscences of African Big Game, *Saturday Evening Post,* December 7, 1929.

14   Ibid.

15   Autobiography, *Adventure,* April 1, 1919.

16   TM to H. H. Howland, March 21, 1919. Bobbs Merrill/Mundy Mss.

17   Cutting from family scrapbook dated February 23, 1895.

18   Publicity Questionnaire, Bobbs Merrill/Mundy Mss.

19   Random Reminiscences of African Big Game Hunting (see above).

20   Letter to A. S. Hoffman from W. R. Foran dated November 4, 1960. Pennsylvania State University.

21   TM to W. H. Gribbon, September 2, 1931.

22 Publicity Questionnaire, Bobbs Merrill/Mundy Mss.

23 Autobiography, *Adventure* (see above)

24 Ibid.

25 Publicity Questionnaire (see above)

26 Autobiography (see above)

27 Ibid.

28 Random Reminiscences of African Big Game Hunting (see above).

29 Autobiography (see above)

30 *Publishers Weekly,* August 11, 1940.

31 Brigadier W. H. Gribbon to Bickerton & Pratt (solicitors) April 21, 1944.
    In view of the circumstances it is perhaps ironic that in 1943 a genealogist
    named Leon White was employed to discover the whereabouts of William
    Lancaster Gribbon or his descendants in order to pay money accruing from
    shares in the Vereeniging Estates Ltd., a South African mining concern,
    which Willie had bought while concerned with Walton & Co.

32 *The Times,* May 6, 1908, and passenger lists in South Africa, February 28,
    1903.

33 Passenger lists in *South Africa,* March 28, 1903.

34 *The Times,* May 6, 1908.

35 Autobiography (see above).

36 Ibid.

37 *The Times,* May 6, 1908.

38 Autobiography (see above).

39 *Manchester Herald,* Connecticut, August 6, 1940.

40 Elephant Hunting for a Living, *Adventure,* July, 1912; Random Remini-
    scences of African Big Game (see above) and Watu — Random Remini-
    scences of Black Africa, *Adventure,* April 1, 1932.

41 *A Cuckoo in Kenya,* W. R. Foran, Hutchinson, London, 1936.

42 Foran's letter to A. S. Hoffman (see above).

43 Evidence at Gribbon v. Gribbon divorce, reported in *The Times Law Report,*
    Vol. XXIV page 160; *The Times,* May 6, 1908; *News of the World,* May 10,
    1908, etc.

44 Ibid.

45 Photostats with writer.

46 *News of the World*, May 10, 1908.

47 *The Times*, May 6, May 9 and May 11, 1908.

48 *New York Times*, October 3, 1909.

49 Ibid.

50 *New York Times*, October 2, 1909.

51 *New York Times*, October 3, 1909.

52 *Nevada State Journal*, August 29, 1923; *Reno Evening Gazette*, August 27, 1923 and *New York Times*, August 28, 1923.

53 *New York Times*, January 20, 1913.

PETER BERRESFORD ELLIS has spent some years researching for a full length biography of Talbot Mundy which is now complete and will be published in 1982. A British author and journalist, one of his recent books was a biography of Rider Haggard, H. RIDER HAGGARD: A VOICE FROM THE INFINITE (Routledge & Kegan Paul, 1978). He gave up the editorship of a weekly British publishing trade journal to become a full time author in 1975 and, under a pseudonym — Peter Tremayne — he also writes fantasy novels.

Mundy house at Anna Maria, Florida.

TALBOT MUNDY

by Dawn Mundy Provost

It was August, 1940, and August in Florida is hot, humid and heavy. A small hurricane had come and gone twenty-four hours previously, when we walked the beach late that night. The wind still blew steadily, tossing phosphorescent wave-crests high. In the turbulence there was a clarity — a feeling of exultation. We walked hand in hand back to the beach house and made love. "Now I think I'll go to sleep," he said.

And he did. In the morning, he was gone — gone to new horizons, to a new consciousness. . . .

Four-fifths of Talbot Mundy's life had been lived, vibrantly, before our paths crossed in the late Fall of 1927. That meeting was against my wishes. My next-door neighbors in Scarsdale, a doctor and his wife, requested that I entertain at the piano for their California house guests — her sister Troy, Larry Trimble, and the Mundys. I was almost seven months pregnant, and hardly felt like performing for strangers. By an ironic twist of fate — or whatever you want to call it — my mother-in-law, who was visiting, insisted that pregnant or not, I should do what the doctor and his wife requested.

So we climbed the hill next door. Etched in my memory is the picture of Talbot Mundy, seated on the floor by the feet of his wife, staring at the roaring fire, the picture of contentment. I wished my marriage were that successful.

Weeks later my baby was born. I lost that child when she was twenty-three days old, due to an intestinal infection. The unexpected blow added to my mounting unhappiness, and to the difference of personal goals that was destroying my marriage.

In the ensuing days, Larry and Troy spent many evenings with us. Larry considered himself an expert in psychology; we were psychoanalyzed, interrogated, cross-examined, challenged, until the discussion of divorce crept in more and more frequently. I also learned that the Mundy marriage, which I had thought so serene, was in fact exceedingly rocky.

As time passed, the combined forces of stress, immaturity, and diverging values took its toll. My husband and I agreed to disagree. Divorce being a difficult road to traverse in any era, my nervousness grew; thoughts became more and more chaotic. I had to get away. My husband decided to go to his mother's for a weekend. I called Troy, who had returned to New York, and asked her to go away with me. She agreed.

By the time I reached her hotel, she had invited Larry. Talbot's wife, hearing of it, insisted Talbot go along for the weekend . . . "he needs a change of scene, he's been working too hard." My conservative New England background reared its head momentarily, but as Talbot Mundy strode out of the hotel, tall, broad-shouldered, salt-and-pepper hair blown by the wind, his smile was so disarming that all resistance vanished.

We headed for the Connecticut shore. After the first hundred miles Larry decided to drive. Definitely in awe of Talbot Mundy — hoping it didn't show — I climbed in the rumble seat beside him.

The next hours opened up a whole new world — his world, the antithesis of mine — of India, where he arrived during a plague, and later when he wandered on his own toward the Khyber Pass and Afghanistan, toward Darjeeling, with the Himalayas and Tibet beyond. It was the first time I heard of the Eastern Teachings, or Mahatmas and their age-old wisdom — all new concepts, mind-expanding.

Two days and many conversations later, while returning to New York, Talbot suddenly grew silent. He stared at me, surprised.

"You know," he said slowly, "I believe I love you more than anything in the world. . . ."

Speechless, inwardly denying, with a sudden intuitive awareness I knew it was true. I didn't know how or why, but it was true for me too. The rest of the day was full of mixed emotions — exhilaration one moment, anxiety, disbelief, the next — he was twenty-four years older, and much wiser.

Once back in New York, Talbot and his wife left for California. Discovering my husband's house was going on the market immediately, I joined Troy in New York, and we shared a hotel suite together. One night in the following weeks, Larry, Troy and I attended a first night at the theater. Between the second and third acts, I became violently ill and had to leave. I couldn't understand

Talbot Mundy

such a malaise; it was utterly foreign to my healthy constitution. Two days later, an interesting letter arrived from California; I realized that exactly at the time of my inexplicable upset, Talbot and his wife were having their final showdown. Coincidence?

When Talbot returned to New York in late June of 1928, one of the first things he did was take my hour and date of birth to astrologer Evangeline Adams for a quick look-see at my horoscope. She had no way of knowing whether it was for male or female. He did not enlighten her. Working briefly, she suddenly went to her files and pulled out Talbot's horoscope: "Extraordinary! So many configurations alike. . . ." The comparison fluffed my ego.

The next thing he did was introduce me to Natacha Rambova, at her designer shop on Fifty-Second Street. It happened to be my birthday, and was memorable to me for many reasons — one of which was another seeming coincidence. I had seen Natacha dance with Rudolph Valentino in Connecticut just prior to my first marriage; with that segment of my experience completed, I was meeting her at the beginning of a new life. Unguessed by either of us at the time, she would play a very important role in my life.

"But," as Talbot often said, "there's no such thing as coincidence."

Our next move — Troy, Larry, Talbot and me — was to rent a small island containing two houses on the St. Lawrence River for six weeks. It was there that the idea of combining my music with Talbot's writing was born — the working title: *A Drama with Music.* Talbot's attorney drew up a contract, and we went to work.

While Talbot typed at a window overlooking the river, I spent days alone in a canoe, drifting, listening, searching for the melodies that would background his ideas. It was also a time when I learned a great deal more about Talbot Mundy, not only through his writings, but from the discussions all four of us had at night. I knew he'd written publicity bits for the publishers of his books, about places he'd been, people and the emotions he'd experienced, which provided not only the backgrounds for his stories, but the characters themselves. And I also knew he'd left a whole lot out. Talbot was extremely reticent about detailing his personal relationships.

He was known as an adventure story writer, but there are few of his manuscripts that do not contain an undercurrent of his philosophy, which was becoming more and more evident to me in his daily life. He was a man of strong opinions, ever-present humor at life's vicissitudes, a man of prodigious faith;

conversely a man with set prejudices, which he yielded with reluctance, and only when convinced he was totally illogical.

He saw the human personality as a circle: "An individual never develops his circle concurrently on all sides. There'll be convex growth in one area — concave depressions in another, where the evolution of self hasn't caught up." It made sense; I hoped my concave depressions weren't showing!

At the end of August, Talbot received word that his library and manuscripts were being shipped to New York. It was time to return to the city. Troy and Larry decided to go on to California — Talbot and I found apartments in an old brownstone on the outskirts of Greenwich Village, just off Fifth Avenue. His studio was three flights up; mine was a room about 45 feet long in what originally must have been the basement, but we didn't notice it then.

There were bookshelves from floor to ceiling in the entrance end, a kitchenette and bath, windows galore — all of which had one-way crinkly glass that created a cathedral atmosphere. It would be a beautiful room for music — Talbot's books filling the end wall (there were no shelves in his studio). So we shopped in auction galleries for effective pieces for our decor, but had hardly started when a complication arose with a publisher.

It had become obvious that Talbot needed an agent, and he was fortunate to find the best almost immediately. Months previously, he had sold a long novel, "Queen Cleopatra," to *Adventure* magazine; the magazine changed editors, and the new man didn't feel the novel fitted his editorial policy. Talbot solved the dilemma by offering to substitute a new manuscript — thus giving himself a deadline to meet.

A long refectory table had been delivered to my apartment. We placed it in the bay window opposite the fireplace — Talbot got his typewriter, rolled five sheets of paper with carbons in place, relaxed in a high-backed chair, eyes half closed. When he could "see — hear — smell — and feel" the scene, the chapter started, and he stayed with it until it was finished. If he became stuck for a word or phrase, he'd flop on a davenport for ten or fifteen minutes, eyes closed — then abruptly back to the typewriter — passage completed. We could function worlds apart during work hours, each wrapped in our own concentration.

Meanwhile, Talbot was receiving long, persuasive letters from a Theosophist friend on Point Loma, California, urging him to return to "where he really belonged." In 1924, he had written *Om, the Secret of Ahbor Valley* in that atmosphere; he'd been concerned with the way the story was going, and told me that halfway through the manuscript, he'd felt the presence of the old lama in the story, who admonished "That won't do, you know, my son . . . " Into the waste-basket went the half-completed manuscript; he started all over again. Despite the pressure, he decided to remain and write in our New York brownstone.

Gradually, we completed the furnishings of both apartments; Talbot chose heavily carved Spanish oak — a desk and high-backed altar chairs for his apartment, and files for his manuscripts. Downstairs, we added an Aeolian Steinway grand piano, Talbot's books filling the end wall, and some Chinese pieces picked up in auction galleries. It was the perfect setting for what Natacha suggested would be an interesting project.

We intended, if possible, to learn what trance mediumship was all about. No table-tipping, no hovering trumpets — rather a serious attempt to discern what, of a positive nature, lay behind the trance state. There were five of us who gathered regularly one night a week: Natacha, Talbot, me, a court stenographer to transcribe notes, and the medium.

Fall and winter evenings . . . light from the fireplace reflected on a gold sari stretched along one wall . . . a small penlight providing the pinpoint of light on the refectory table for note-taking behind the medium's chair; the room created the atmosphere we needed.

Natacha was a student of comparative religions, ancient Egyptian culture, and the writings of Helena Petrovna Blavatsky (H.P.B), the founder of Theoso-phy. Talbot had been exposed to the Church of England, the Eastern Teachings and Mahatmas, Christian Science and Mary Baker Eddy, Theosophy at Point Loma, and the writings of H.P.B. and her teachers — in that order. I had stumbled around, knowing only that my Congregational Church background left many questions unanswered.

Our mood attracted intelligent and intensely interesting discussions about life after "death," bringing most often a voice identifying itself as H.P.B. Natacha and Talbot were the judges of its authenticity; the statements made, the manner in which they were worded, the personality traits that seeped through, all seemed genuine.

Occasionally we invited guests. Some were open-minded, interested — others rejected what we sought. It didn't matter whether the disbelief was verbal or subconscious — those particular evenings were a fiasco. We learned quickly — became a closed corporation, so to speak.

There was one session that stands out cameo-clear; Natacha's attorney and good friend was seriously ill, and had been taken unconscious to the hospital. Natacha asked for help; an awareness of power filled the room — we all felt it

— intense, electric, exploding in flashes of blue light. A voice intoned: "Ma-ry Ba-ker Ed-dy." A healing. A prayer. Silence.

It makes no difference who or what the manifestation was; it accomplished results. Later that night Natacha learned from a nurse in the hospital that at the precise moment of our experience (all times were written in our transcribed notes) the patient suddenly gained consciousness. . . . "Where is she . . . the white-haired little lady . . . where did she go?"

I began having psychic experiences, usually when near or entering the sleep state. The first one made my blood run cold. Six feet above my head appeared a round iron grating shaped like a cover. Lying on cold, damp ground, I stared up at the dim light, growing brighter with each plodding footstep that approached across an echoing courtyard. It was ancient Rome. . . . I was a prisoner, not Roman, something else . . . terrified. Consciousness found me bolt upright in bed, shivering, searching for the overhead grating. Sleep ended abruptly.

Another occurrence was of being drawn up through the case of the grand piano opposite my bed, finding myself on a sunlit plateau above a river, peering around a rock formation. Enormous slabs lay all around. A short distance away stood a tall Egyptian, magnificently attired in a short white tunic, heavily ornamented with gold trim. Only a glimpse — but I knew he was the one this life called Talbot.

These reactions were obviously spawned by the evening sessions, and were a relatively small part of our lives. Days were full, each of us working, occasionally interrupted by trips uptown for conferences with Talbot's agent or his attorney, through whom he was attempting to straighten out his marital tangle. My divorce had come through promptly the preceding Fall.

One day a completely unexpected situation cropped up; a man, unknown to him, phoned and asked for an appointment. It took place in Talbot's apartment, and when he came to tell me about it, he was more angry than I'd ever seen him. "Son of a bitch!"

"What happened?"

"Craven's attorney sent him." . . . Inez Craven, Talbot's wife, divorced in New York after their arrival in America. . . . "He threatened to put me in jail."

"Why, for heaven's sake?"

"Because I'm behind in alimony payments. . . . I knew that. Told him to go ahead . . . if he did, I'd be damned if I'd ever write another word!"

"Did he believe you?"

"Don't know. He'll phone tomorrow to see if I come up with a satisfactory compromise." He lighted a cigarette. "Actually, he wasn't a bad chap. Only did what he was paid to do."

That problem was straightened out satisfactorily. By Spring of 1929, the manuscript debt was paid, and with a book ahead — COCK O' THE NORTH — Talbot decided we'd go to Europe. He had his reasons — or his alibi, as the case might be; there was an English agent to convince that a group of previously completed short stories should be the next English book publication. Talbot was an enthusiastic convincer, and won most of his attempts.

The medium was to accompany us to Europe, Talbot curious to observe his reactions. We sailed on a passenger-carrying freighter, mostly cargo, only twelve staterooms. It was like having a private yacht, slow by comparison to the big liners, but immense fun, all new to me.

Overcast, cold and windy, the ship rolled and pitched toward England, with Talbot and me on deck most of the time. One early morning, on the deck outside my stateroom, he called through the port: "Wake up! We've reached the south coast of England, and we'll soon be off the coast where Caesar landed!"

Our ship followed the Thames to London . . . and my first impression of England contained the Romans, and the ancient land of Briton of the *Tros* stories, as well as the London of stately buildings, Buckingham Palace, Westminster Abbey, the Tower, and famous restaurants, as full of history as of good food. Talbot loved his native land, and knew its history intimately.

We took bus trips to outlying districts, always seated on the top deck. On one of those trips, I caught a high heel in the top step, and cascaded to the bottom. My knee hurt savagely. Talbot reached for my hand, and in less than a minute, the pain vanished. I do not know whether he had the power to heal others, but he could and did heal me when the need was urgent.

We left London by train for Paris, where our stay was brief; then on to Rome. The medium decided on a side trip to Switzerland, and we made plans to meet later on. In Rome, the first requisite was a car with driver, and a guide. Talbot found a moonlighting college professor who spoke excellent English; he was a most devout Catholic. . . . those first days, interspersed with Roman ruins, we saw more churches than we knew existed, including the Vatican and Sistine Chapel, a memory which erased all the weariness.

The next morning, we opted for ancient Rome . . . the Forum, Caesar's Rome. Again I saw through talbot's eyes, as his character Tros of Samothrace lived it: the contrasts — on one hand, the ancient splendor and trappings of the wealthy, with their captured slaves from all nations — the poverty and squalor of the masses, and the narrow streets where they rioted — the arena where Christians died, and gladiators fought to the death — the dungeons where the doomed were incarcerated until it was their time to die. I kept searching for a round iron grid overhead . . . the grid of my nightmare . . . but it wasn't there.

Lunch was a welcome interlude, high on a hill overlooking the city; delicious food, and a very mellow wine. I forgot all about that grid. Then we returned to an ancient prison near the Forum. It was a dungeon below ground; in recent centuries, a wooden church had been erected over it. It was a stark, wood-walled room, and as we crossed it, I became aware of tiny blue-light explosions all around, which couldn't come from the only light in the room, an unshielded bulb which glared dead white. The blue light puzzled me; why was I seeing it?

On the left, a stairway led down to the dungeon, and as we reached the bottom the guide struck a huge iron double door, which gave off a hollow sound.

"In Caesar's day they tossed prisoners through here — into the cloaca maximus, the main sewer of ancient Rome."

Suddenly the dungeon teemed with horror — oppressive, claustrophobic, an area to abandon quickly. Talbot, ascending the stairs, grabbed the handrail — frozen in midstride — his face blanched, staring at a spot midway across the cell. I followed his gaze — the round iron grid! Hypnotized, it took all my self-control to keep from lying down on the dirt floor, to re-live the nightmare. Neither of us spoke until the guide had preceded us up and out of the prison.

"Talbot — !"

"I saw myself hanging by a rope — being strangled and dropped through that hole — I felt it!" He was rubbing his throat.

"The grid! It's the same — in my nightmare — but *you* weren't part of it . . ."

"Perhaps different times — different happenings — same place."

We discussed it in its meagre detail later, but came up with no further understanding. It was life that happened centuries in the past. . . .

After a short visit to Naples, Talbot hired a car to drive us up the coast of Italy, along a beautiful winding drive skirting the southern end of Europe — cliffs on one side, the blue Mediterranean on the other — through Monte Carlo, Nice, stopping finally at Juanles-Pins to pay a courtesy call on Natacha's mother. There the medium joined us. Then back to England, and the ship that had brought us over weeks before.

When Talbot and I arrived back in New York in early September of 1929, following that trip to Europe, the apartments seemed depressingly dark after all the outdoors and sunshine. Our leases were up, so we moved to the Master Building, a tall new apartment hotel on Riverside Drive. Talbot chose an eighteenth floor balconied apartment facing south; around the corner was a smaller one facing west, directly over the Hudson — sunlight and air sufficient to suit anyone. Natacha's lease expired at the same time, so she joined us, taking a suite three floors higher. Soon after, the medium decided to tag along.

The Roerich Museum occupied the lower floors of the building, filled with eye-arresting paintings by Nicholas Roerich. At showings, Roerich dominated the room — a small man with an exceptionally quiet voice, who exuded an air of mystery — a personification of one of his own paintings of a Tibetan mystic.

In this new environment Talbot's days began at three a.m. — a cup of coffee beside him, the usual five sheets of paper with carbon in the typewriter — the usual hours of work, until a chapter was finished. I worked on music in my own apartment.

There was much other work to be done, readying a group of short stories for publication in England. After a disastrous experience with a public stenographer — pages and paragraphs out of sequence — I persuaded him to let me have a try at it. It was easy to make the transition from piano keyboard to typewriter . . . except that my feet continually searched for pedals!

At night we carried on the weekly sessions started on Ninth Street. There were two instances in which Talbot's brother, a Brigadier General, introduced himself through the medium, telling of his death in Egypt. The morning after the second "appearance," the medium stopped at Talbot's apartment with the morning mail, and handed him a thick letter with English postage. As he left, Talbot plumped into a chair, a quizzical expression on his face. "Haven't seen the handwriting in fifteen years, but I'd recognize it anywhere. My brother Harold's . . . very *much* alive!"

After that, we attempted to have the medium remain conscious, not allowing him to go into a trance. That produced weird results, the final one when he went suddenly beserk, and made a headlong dash for the open door to the balcony. It was eighteen floors to the street below; being nearest the door, I threw myself in front of him; his strength was incredible, but the jolt stopped him. He returned to his chair, obviously confused. The experience sobered all of us.

In the following months, we were often joined by Roerich's son, Svetislov, who was painting a portrait of Natacha. The four of us dined, more often than not, either in Talbot's apartment or in Svetie's at the top of the tower. There were evenings with friends . . . Leslie Grant and her husband R. T. M. Scott . . . Conrad Bercovici . . . Elmer Davis and his wife in their New York apartment, and later a visit to their summer home on the Sound. There were large gatherings in Svetie's apartment: bookstore owners, Russians, Poles, celebrities from the art or theatre world, each party containing a diversity of individuals. When Natacha was otherwise engaged, Svetie, Talbot and I occasionally took in the fights at Madison Square Garden.

Just before Christmas the second year, the management of the museum asked Talbot to go to London at their expense; Nicholas Roerich was attempting to get into India, but neither Washington nor London had seen fit to grant him a visa. No one could find out why. For some reason of his own, Roerich felt that Talbot could prevail on the British authorities. Talbot wasn't convinced; but, even though the Christmas holiday was fast approaching, he agreed to go.

We had an hilarious day dreaming up a code by which Talbot's accomplishment — favorable or otherwise — could be transmitted by cable back to New York. "I'll send my cables to Dawn — that way it'll be less official, in case the British check up." The museum people didn't like it, but that's the way it was.

Talbot wasn't gone over fifteen days, but the pressure became intense as first the museum staff, then Natacha and Svetie, grew pessimistic. They all agreed it had been a foolhardy mission — obviously Talbot could do nothing. Being prejudiced, I disagreed. Finally, a telephone call came through for me at the museum office, monitored by all concerned — Talbot had succeeded! The museum was later notified that Roerich had entered India, and was on his way to his destination.

On cloud nine, I met the steamship *Aquitania;* it was wonderful to see Talbot striding toward me . . . it felt as if he'd been gone months. Then I noticed the striking brunette beside him; they'd met aboard ship — she was enroute to the West Coast — and Talbot had offered to put her up during her stay in New York. I volunteered quickly — she would be *my* guest!

Thus I learned that some of the critics of Talbot's books weren't necessarily right: he did like women, particularly if they were good looking and intelligent . . . and the attraction was mutual. After six weeks, the lady left.

Months passed, and by the Spring of '31, the Depression was gaining frightening momentum. Natacha had been uneasy about conditions in the United

States for some time, feeling that a revolution of some sort was unavoidable. She decided to close her shop, and go to Juan-les-Pins, to continue with a brand of cosmetics her step-father, Richard Hudnut, had urged her to manufacture. At dinner, pros and cons were discussed endlessly; we decided I would accompany Natacha to Europe. . . . Talbot would follow later. I wrote my family; two nights later, the plans took an unexpected turn when Talbot said "Believe I'll go to Yucatan first, then — "

Natacha interrupted: "Wasn't that where you were married last time?"

"Right. A divorce now would speed up the settlement, be an accomplished fact. . . . "

Natacha was laughing, looking first at Talbot, then at me. "Why don't you two . . . ?"

"My God, yes! How about it, Dawn? You come with me."

Within a week, we three moved out of the Roerich Building; I stayed with Natacha temporarily in a small apartment over her shop. . . . Talbot went to the Algonquin Hotel.

We almost didn't make it the day the Morro Castle sailed. Talbot was to call for me and my luggage on his way to the ship . . . but he didn't show up. I finally phoned the hotel; he was completely hung over from a farewell party the night before. (Natacha and I were luckier — we had dined at Norman Bel Geddes' apartment, and had come away somewhat better off.)

"Do you *want* to go?"

"God, yes. I — I'm not packed . . . "

"Be there." Manhandling my trunk down three flights of stairs, I hailed a taxi and arrived at Talbot's room breathless.

"Sorry. It really hit me." He looked it.

I packed. He combed rumpled hair and put on a tie slightly askew. A bellhop helped close his bags, and we flew through the lobby to my waiting taxi. Aboard ship, shortly after sailing, we met and went to the promenade deck where he decided to balance his checkbook — ignored for the past week while checks continued to flow.

It was an exciting voyage, with my Natacha Rambova trousseau and the distinguished-looking man who was my constant companion. A day in Cuba, then on to Progresso, in those days the "port" of Yucatan. A ship had to stand miles off the beach because of the shallowness of the Gulf of Mexico, and there occurred a musical comedy transfer between ship and shore. A small coastwise tug, crewed by ten gold-braided officers and two crewmen, who solemnly perused our passports, gave us landing slips, and with stolid dignity escorted those going ashore aboard the tiny tug. As it pulled away from the massive liner, it gave two high-pitched toots reminiscent of the "Little Engine That Could." Laughter from the liner's deck followed us ashore. . . .

In Merida, about twelve kilometers inland, we settled into a massive old hacienda, once a governor's mansion, now converted into a hotel. Ushered into a large bright room that was to be mine, I heard a slithering behind me on the stone floor, and turned to see a three inch-long scorpion, armored like a lobster, coming toward me. My yelp was heard in the inner courtyard below. I was transferred immediately to a smaller room, hopefully without scorpions; Talbot fared better — he never even saw one in his room.

Having seen the American Consul to set in motion the necessary legal machinery for Talbot's divorce, we spent much time in the Museum and in visiting ancient ruins. Wherever we went, the thought uppermost in Talbot's mind was the sequel to the *Tros* stories — Tros's long dreamed of voyage around the world. It would include this ancient land of the Mayas — about which he'd already done a great deal of research — as one segment of the voyage. It was the one book he wanted to write, the one book he would have written had time allowed.

We went to Chichen Itza, a four a.m., four-hour train ride followed by a jaunt across country in an ancient Ford truck, through fly belts where the flies were dragons with teeth, to the impressively massive Mayan ruins. Later, on to the Sacrificial Pool, and a sister pool where, when we swam, our hands were invisible an inch below the surface because of the silt and left mold of centuries from the overhanging jungle. Another trip to Uxmal, and the dizzying climb up painfully narrow stairs, to the top of the pyramid, which Talbot took in easy strides; then, for me, the terrifying descent, totally undignified . . . sitting down one step at a time, all the way to the bottom.

There was the day we were taken by Yucatecan acquaintances to a hacienda where tall trees, laden with giant avocados, overhung the terrace. We swam in an arched swimming pool built five hundred years before and drank tequila. Talbot was strongly tempted to buy the place, until he learned that no foreigner could own land in such close proximity to the Gulf, without a Mexican partner.

Returning to the hotel, Talbot was greeted by a cable saying that the draft he'd drawn on his bank some days previously couldn't be honored, because of "insufficient funds."

"What the devil! You saw me balance the checkbook on the Morro Castle. Here — go over it. I'll send some wires."

The error wasn't hard to find; two pages had stuck together, thus six checks had not been deducted from the balance. His wires brought the needed funds, but henceforth, the responsibility for the checkbook was mine.

Meanwhile, the American Consul told us that six weeks residency was required for a divorce in Yucatan, but in the neighboring state of Campeche, we'd already completed the necessary Mexican residence.

"You divorced number three here in Yucatan?"

"She threatened to have my letters read in court."

"And married my predecessor . . . "

"Right. So now a divorce in Campeche, and marry . . . "

"Number five! Boy, what a record!"

"Afraid?" Laughing.

"No way."

"The consul will accompany us, and attend to all details and consular stamps. It's legal, not only in the United States, but anywhere."

So once again we took the four a.m. train — it seems all trains in Merida departed at four a.m. — this time in a southwesterly direction. It was hot and dusty when we arrived at high noon, and found the only hotel where we could lunch. Then on to the courthouse.

Divorce was granted in front of the judge's bench; Talbot was escorted to the other end of the room, where the judge again appeared and our witnesses and the consul stood. My witness was a young man who had checked the record — knew my birthplace was Connecticut — and explained that because his cousin had attended Yale, he was an old and good friend. So there, July 31st, 1931, at 1:30 P.M. we were married.

Talbot was very quiet, very serious. His eyes held mine throughout the ceremony, and when he put the ring on my finger and kissed me, his eyes were misty. Companion, friend, lover, teacher, and now husband, he was all these to me, and for all time would continue to be. . . .

Back in Merida, Talbot invited all the people we'd met to a celebration: the consul, American engineers on assignment in Mexico, musicians who serenaded with guitars, and the Yucatecans who'd befriended us these past weeks — all men, since no Yucatecan women were seen in public restaurants. A perfect end to a perfect day.

We caught the Morro Castle on her next trip down and were promptly invited to the captain's table. In Vera Cruz, we made one brief trip ashore; the city was dirty and foul-smelling in sharp contrast to Merida, where everything was spotlessly clean. Heading back to New York, the voyage was completed in perfect weather.

We were deeply saddened when, years later, the Morro Castle burned to a hulk, and passengers and captain died. A tragic end to a beautiful, and fondly-remembered, ship . . .

Our stay at the Algonquin was brief — finances needed recouping. With a telegram from Natacha saying she was going on a yachting trip in the Mediterranean, we took the train to Connecticut to introduce the new son-in-law to a very square dad. Mother and Talbot had met twice in New York and gotten along famously, as did the three of them from then on.

After a few months work, part of it at a lake where the family owned a cottage, we bought a car and headed for the Gulf Coast of Florida. Talbot didn't like to drive — "rather handle horses" — but I did. We found a small cottage on the outskirts of St. Petersburg; even though winter had come, we took our lunch to the beach and swam every day. It was a period of lazy vacation — Talbot sunburned red, and I tanned deeply.

A letter from Natacha got us moving again; she was now living in Mallorca, Spain, modernizing old houses in a village called Genova, outside Palma. "Come on over. I've got just the place for you."

Talbot was also in correspondence with Troy in California, and on learning our plans, she decided to accompany us. So it was back to Connecticut to re-pack clothes, typewriters, and two Pekinese pups . . . then a quick turnaround to pick up Troy in New York and continue on to Baltimore, to load the car on a ship.

Our destination was Hamburg. Talbot would leave the ship in Cherbourg to make a quick business trip to London, while we went on, unloaded the car and dogs, and awaited his arrival.

We landed in Hamburg the day prior to the last national election that Hitler lost. Times were difficult, the German representative of the Royal Automobile Club said. He had overseen the unloading of the car, and guided us to a hotel and restaurant where he joined us for lunch. He refused to discuss politics in public, and kept glancing furtively over his shoulder. We'd been invited by one of the ship's officers to dinner that night, and afterward he escorted us to a below-sidewalk bar and dancehall frequented by homosexuals and transvestites. We were instructed to drink coffee . . . show no surprise . . . attract no attention. It was a very proper, almost pedantic, coffee hour.

Within twenty-four hours Talbot joined us and we started for Spain. Our itinerary took us on narrow brick roads, where gasoline pumps were rare, and traffic was an occasional farm wagon. Through picturesque German villages of medieval times, each house closely grouped to its neighbor, with piles of manure in front; south to the Quedlinburg of Talbot's youth, and on to Heidelburg. Wherever we stopped in small towns, people talked of hard times. One innkeeper, having served over-generous portions of excellent food and the ever-present good German beer, complained bitterly about people starving. "Me — thirty pounds gone — " and at least two hundred remained.

On April 23rd, 1932, Talbot bought a German National Lottery ticket. "It'll be lucky. Want to bet?" There were no takers. It was his birthday.

Soon we were across the French border and down through the countryside to Perpignan, below which we entered Spain. In Barcelona, there was a modern overnight ferry designed by Norman Bel Geddes, and much more eye-pleasing than those at home. The next morning we reached our destination, Palma de Mallorca.

Natacha greeted us with a big surprise: "My husband, Alvaro de Urzaiz." Slim, black-haired, and charming — Natacha more beautiful than ever — they made a striking couple. Alvaro's mother had been a lady-in-waiting to the Queen, and had educated him in England, in preparation for his becoming a Spanish naval officer. But times had changed, and Spain was in the midst of political upheaval which eventually would lead to war — and dictatorship. Natacha met Alvaro when he captained the yacht on which she'd been a guest, and spotted his deep depression. He felt his life a complete waste; she convinced him otherwise. They married and became a partnership in the renovations at Genova.

There was no sign of depression now, as they led the way out of Palma, up winding dirt roads to the house that perched high on a mountain overlooking the Mediterranean, a couple of miles away. Our house, with a broad terrace across the front, was completely renovated inside, but the huge water tank, which would become another terrace on completion, was still in the process of building. All water would be trucked in from Palma. Natacha had installed a Mallorquin couple, the wife Magdalena to cook and clean, the husband to keep the car polished in exchange for food and lodging.

Our two Pekinese, bored and edgy from the close proximity of ship and car, immediately staked out private domains. Ping, the larger, with red luxuriant feathers that touched the floor, adopted Magdalena, and retired huffily to her quarters. Babuji, the toy brown-and-white, lorded it over the rest of the house.

Talbot's studio was on the lower level under the terrace, with the Mediterranean sparkling inspiration in the distance; a narrow extension of the terrace ran along the side of the house to the bedroom where my typewriter was installed, with a vista of both sea and an enormous cactus alongside, which turned orange-gold in the sunsets.

Life gradually became normal. In the beginning, my Spanish was non-existent; Magdalena understood no English, but became a very good teacher. I'd point to things — trees, wall, ground, food — "Que est esta?" She'd name it, and slowly there grew enough vocabulary for me to run a house. After shopping twice with her for food, she came to me, unhappy; the senora was being cheated. If the senor and senora would allow, and give her the money, she would buy the groceries. It worked wonders on the grocery bills.

There were amusing interludes. Water tank completed, Talbot prepared a welcome hot tub. Just before my foot touched the water, I looked more closely. "It's alive!" The water was crowded with wigglers — someone had forgotten to put charcoal in the watertank.

Cows couldn't live on the mountainside; instead, a herd of goats was driven early each morning to the gate, and milked into the household pitcher. There was no refrigeration; food was stored in a wired enclosure that allowed air to circulate, but precluded leftovers.

Not far from us, one of Natacha's friends lived in another renovated house, clinging to the side of a ravine. Below was a septic tank, which backed up disastrously during a party one night. Natacha fumed: "These damn natives! They believe that what they leave *out* is an improvement on the design. They'll learn. It'll be fixed tomorrow."

There were small rocky coves to swim in, the Mediterranean degrees colder in summer than Florida in winter. There were trips to take — one to the end of the island, where a fashionable hotel served delicious food and drinks. To get there, we all piled in our car and edged up and down the dirt switchbacks that threaded through and over the mountains. Sometimes the driving, particularly at night, was a bit hairy. There was a monastery high on a hill, where George Sand and Chopin had lived, and where now friends of Natacha and Alvaro entertained.

During the days, the sound of typewriters was continuous. Stories went off

Seated, left to right:
   Talbot Mundy, Dawn Mundy, Natacha Rambova
Standing:
   Alvaro de Urzaiz.

to New York, but they were slow in selling. Being three thousand miles away from the market was a bit grim, and to further complicate things, an heir was expected in the Mundy family. Dawn was pregnant, and Talbot was ecstatic — we'd host a celebration to announce the good news. In the midst of planning, the mail arrived; Talbot's German lottery ticket had won almost two hundred dollars. "I told you I'd be lucky!"

We rounded up Natacha, Alvaro and a few others; that night, with local wines and cheeses, an enormous canned ham from Swift, and Black Label scotch (at a dollar and a half a quart), Talbot made his announcement — even more expansive and enthusiastic than ever, if that were possible.

Shortly afterward, Troy decided to return to California — the hot sun of the Balearics was too much for her, she said. It might also have been that she was lonely, or the discussions among Alvaro, Natacha and Talbot bored her. Talbot had just finished a non-fiction book, which he called for the time being *Thus Spake the Devil,* under the non de plume of Malloy Grayson, which brought forth all his strong dislikes of bureaucracy, lawyers, doctors, and the Catholic Church. (Note: It did not sell. Later, in Florida, T.M. completely rewrote it — with the same result. It became the basis for *I Say Sunrise* issued after his death.) Alvaro was a staunch Catholic. Talbot could be very bull-headed, even for one born under the sign of Taurus, and usually pursued his arguments to their extremes.

We saw Troy off on the ferry, looking very blond and attractive standing on the deck. It seemed strange to see her leave, she'd been so much a part of our lives.

Talbot returned to writing fiction, but made time to send for circulars from Swiss and French clinics, and from a small private hospital outside London run by Theosophists. Alvaro suggested an excellent clinic in Palma owned by two surgeon brothers, which we agreed to because of its proximity. So we settled into Fall, working and contented.

Unexpectedly, the Spanish government changed our decision; in December, they proclaimed that on the first of January, all foreign cars would be taxed on original cost, in gold. That we could not afford. We took the car to Palma's best garage, had it tuned and everything possible done to prepare for the trip to England. The mechanics added a touch of their own: all the chrome was greased to prevent corrosion on the hundred-mile ferry trip to Barcelona, and a Cadillac in those days had a whale of a lot of chrome, including the spotlight and extra driving lights.

Two days after Christmas, 1932, packed to the roof, the two Pekes astride the accumulated luggage — we said goodbye to Magdalena, to Natacha and Alvaro, and headed for the ferry. Car safely aboard, we watched pigs being loaded for market, so overweight that they had to be carried aboard in slings, to protect fragile legs and ankles. The stench was unbelievable.

Ashore in Barcelona, our first priority was good gasoline. For months, we'd had to use five-gallon tins of Russian gasoline, the only available fuel in Mallorca — it made a motor balk at the slightest hill. We learned that the direct route north through Perpignan and France was flooded, leaving only the longer road across Spain, south of the Pyrenees. The trip began uneventfully, then the first tire blew, and we discovered the tire tool had rusted, and would no longer remove the lugs. A friendly truckdriver solved that dilemma . . . then a second tire went flat as we stopped some miles from a village, to eat the lunch Magdalena had prepared for us. Eventually help arrived from the village, but we had to stay overnight to get tire and tool repaired. Two more blew before we reached Dieppe, where we would ferry across to New Haven.

In Dieppe, we left the pups with a vet, rather than quarantine them for six months in England.

Thus we arrived in left-hand drive country; I was just beginning to feel confident after twenty miles, when . . . *"Could* we go a little faster? We've got to reach London tonight."

Speedometer registered 18 mph . . . we moved out.

There was a fifth blown tire in the midst of London traffic, but we reached the town of Blackheath that night, and the flat near the hospital which the doctors had graciously arranged for us. We were grateful for the darkness; the car was a mess, greased chrome covered with mud, two empty fenderwells which had contained the tires which blew, and the chrome radiator emblem rusted off, leaving a hole.

Nature was kind; it snowed for two days, covering the sight, and there the Cadillac stood for two months. We walked to and from the clinic, and Talbot took busses to London. Memories from that interim include the coldest sheets in the world, impenetrable fog from a third floor window, and a tiny gas fire to warm the feet.

We were still undecided about names; in Mallorca, there had been such an abundance of correspondence with both the New York and London agents that Talbot had proclaimed "If it's a boy, it'll be 101 Park Avenue . . . if a girl, Henrietta Street!"

Little Hall, Eversley, Hampshire, England; home of Brigadier W. H. Gribbon.

The baby was a girl . . . stillborn.

That night, at my request, the nurse brought her to me and left us alone. Dressed in her going-home clothes, she was unbelievably lovely, dark-lashed, curly haired, asleep never to waken. Talbot found us. In silence, we watched. . .

He returned to the flat and started a book, which was as yet untitled. Later he brought some completed material for me to read. The heroine's name was Henrietta. "It's the only way I can express how I feel, Dawn."

I understood. . . .

An invitation came to visit relatives of Talbot's at their country home in Surrey. As soon as I was allowed to drive, we left Blackheath — and arrived looking like a worn-out gypsy caravan. The butler hurriedly extricated the needed luggage — then moved the car to a closed garage, away from the house and out of sight.

Our gracious hosts gave no inkling of how they felt about our appearance, but we knew. The next morning, we located the nearest garage and set out to correct the impression; hours later, with new tires, a wash and polish, radiator emblem back in position, we returned. From that point on, when anyone went anywhere, it was by request in the American car.

It was an impressive estate with acres of manicured lawns and gardens, onto which opened French doors from a most unexpected Chinese drawing room. Black-walled, with gold recessed ceiling — black drapes — an exquisite gold-medallioned Chinese figure centered in each hanging — and furniture in perfect taste, grouped around a fireplace. Apart from the main house was an old guesthouse with mullioned windows in a circular wall, coverted into a radio and music room with a grand piano. Upstairs a ping-pong table, my introduction to the sport; the first day, we played forty-two games. Returning exhausted to the drawing room for tea, I was introduced — much to Talbot's amusement — as "our little American cousin," with the slight flavor of condescension of well-born British toward native Americans. It was difficult not to grin, with Talbot's eyes on me.

Talbot was assigned a guest bedroom to work in, where he set up his typewriter, closed the door, and went to work on the manuscript FULL MOON, started in Blackheath. How he managed to complete the novel in that structured life, I don't know. Breakfasts no one spoke; everyone but me read the racing news from his favorite newspaper, then made a beeline for the telephone to post his bet. Luncheon, with pitchers of beer . . . afternoon tea, a time to relax until the dressing gong rang, then upstairs to prepare for dinner with, naturally, cocktails first. Always two kinds of wine with dinner, followed by brandy, coffee in the drawing room, and whatever else anyone desired. Despite the distractions, Talbot was able to complete his novel.

It was an interlude offered by generous and sympathetic friends, which blunted the loss of our child and brought us into the present. One special day, Talbot and I drove to his brother's, where two whose lives had travelled such divergent ways picked up their ties of friendship. Talbot enlivened the afternoon with the description of the medium's error, of the Brigadier's demise, and sudden resurrection via letter. Harold was destined to do a mansize job in a war still six years in the future. . . .

Then it was time to leave Surrey; a quick trip to pick up the pups and a Norway, Maine friend of Talbot's now married to a Frenchman and living in Paris. The four of us drove to Marseilles to put the car on the Dollar Line, the least expensive way home. After a farewell bottle of wine, Talbot and I boarded the ship and decided to go on the wagon, after all those weeks of lavish living. . .

We arrived in New York in the Summer of 1933. Prohibition was ending and beer was legal — signs shouted it all the way along the turnpike to Connecticut. We were welcomed with open arms by my family, and once again we settled down to work. But late that Fall, wanderlust again seized Talbot; we arrived at a rented cottage, sight unseen, on Casey's key on the Gulf Coast of Florida. It was more a shack than a cottage, on an out-of-this-world island of dirt roads which wound through palms and jungle; no running water, no electricity or telephones, and a "philosopher's box" . . . the outhouse on a walkway over the bay, exceeding chilly on winter nights.

When we moved our luggage in, the outlook was discouraging; a dark brown, dark-cornered environment with cockroaches. But the beauty of the wide white beach in front, and the blue of the bay behind, sent us to the paintstore. By the end of the week, the old wreck had Chinese doorways and painted floors, and an absence of anything that crawled. A rented baby grand provided the music Talbot loved, and we were ready to settle down.

At long last, I too discovered that four a.m. was the perfect hour for uninterrupted work; it was my job to type the book manuscript of *Tros of Samothrace*, with Talbot inserting any necessary connective passages, and the "Sayings" which were such an important part of the book.

Through Talbot's voluminous correspondence, we made many friends. One, a fan, had begged to make the trip with us; she was an actress who had

BRANDT & BRANDT

101 PARK AVENUE, NEW YORK

Telephone AShland 4-5890

November 30, 1938

Mr. Talbot Mundy,
Seven Gables,
Anna Maria,
Florida.

Dear Dawn and Talbot:

This letter is of no business importance whatsoever. It's simply to say that every now and then
I look up and think of you two and hope you're happy
and that the damn radio isn't running you too ragged.
I have a slight nostalgia for the days when you
could be doing me a bit of fiction now and again.
How about it?

Love always.

As ever,

Carl Brandt:VR

March 25th 1914.

Dear Jeff.

This first copy of the first edition of my first book goes off to you ten minutes after I received it. But for you and your yeoman aid when I most needed it the book could never have been written. This goes "lest we forget."

Yours until the numbers go up on the big board

Talbot Mundy

Unique inscription to Jeff (Hanley) in the first copy of Mundy's first book, now in the library of Charles N. Brown. Photograph by Charles N. Brown.

solar heaters on the spacious garage roof for hot water (Florida had them way back *then!*), picture windows facing the Gulf both upstairs and down, the entire house fitted with venetian blinds to control the glare, and an extra bathroom in one of the master bedrooms.

Each morning, Talbot went downstairs early to listen to the morning broadcasts from Europe; in early '39, war appeared inevitable, and it weighed heavily on him. He was working on what was to be his last book, *Old Ugly Face* . . . the only one he ever did in longhand. "It's the only way it'll come. . . ."

I'd submit typed pages, which he would hone and polish and rephrase, then I'd re-type them over and over again. The scripts were done at night now, and they continued almost year-round.

We sought a mortgage on the house — repairs had amounted to more than we'd expected — and the savings and loan asked us to get life insurance as extra collateral. We crossed the street to the local medical building, and located a doctor for what we thought was a routine physical exam. The charming old G.P. discovered the cause of Talbot's weight loss immediately: diabetes.

He wanted to start insulin shots on the spot, but Talbot had an intense antipathy to hyperdermic needles. "Let's try a diet for a week." At home, we searched the dictionary to learn what diabetes *was*, and, thinking we knew, altered the diet a bit, cutting here and there, in an attempt to speed recovery. A disastrously wrong thing to do!

On the next visit, the doctor prepared a syringe out of Talbot's sight, all the while discussing the mounting unrest in Europe. He turned, needle held behind him, pushed up Talbot's short sleeve and injected the insulin in one motion, before Talbot realized what was happening. "I refuse to take responsibility for your life, Mr. Mundy." A blood test had shown Talbot on the brink of a diabetic coma; it was done . . . the lion was tamed . . . he'd had a shot!

We bought books and medical supplies and returned to the island to educate ourselves — primarily me. It took three months to bring him back to normal; four tests a day, about a thousand varied menus to satisfy the whims of a man on a diet, unused to illness. I gave the shot early each morning, and never ceased being fearful of hitting a vein, so when we went for our swim, there was always a lump of sugar with me in a hidden container, just in case. But luck held.

He even began gaining weight. We could go to New York, eat in restaurants, and no one guessed. After all the study of food values and the weighing of portions, I knew the diet by heart; Talbot would say "How about . . . ?" I'd counter with "wouldn't so-and-so be better?" and it all worked out smoothly.

Old Ugly Face completed and published, we invited the family to come live in the spacious quarters we had prepared for them. Ruddy-cheeked and healthy again, Talbot's normal good humor reasserted itself, but he was deeply troubled when war broke out in Europe, although he'd forseen it before some of his correspondants in London did. We never missed foreign broadcasts, listened to Mussolini and Hitler — the raucous egomania of the latter very apparent over radio — and the contrasting "blood, sweat, and tears" speech of Winston Churchill.

The first weekend of August, 1940, we were finishing a radio script late at night; Talbot's desk faced the open doors of the workroom, to the terrace . . . my long typing table eased up to his desk, making an ell. During a lull in dictation I glanced out the door, and became transfixed: in the darkness, a gleaming golden Buddha about three feet tall faced me, and in front of it, a black-robed hooded figure suddenly appeared, arms outstretched. For an interminable moment, I froze . . . recognized . . . denied — glanced at Talbot — had he seen. He was finishing a game of solitaire, looking down at the cards. I stole a sideways glance — the terrace was empty. I blanked out the strange phenomenon and wouldn't remember it again for forty-eight hours. Talbot finished dictating the *Jack Armstrong* script, and discussed how the next one would open.

A small hurricane went through during the night, the "eye" missing us directly. The next day was Sunday. After breakfast, stretched out on a chaise lounge in the workroom, Talbot said:

"Dawn, I'm weary — more weary than I've ever been. Only two more scripts to go on this sequence. The new five-year agreement has gone off and we'll have a breather before buckling down to next year's program."

"Let's take a vacation — go somewhere."

"I'd like that. But let's wait and decide where, tomorrow."

We discussed the non-fiction manuscript that had never sold. It was my belief that he'd tried to cover too much ground, used the book to argue his personal antipathies, and buried the main theme. He listened attentively. Then:

"I agree. So *you* cut it. When you're finished, show it to me."

I was astounded. He'd never said anything like that to me. While he read that afternoon, I completed the future year's budget — the last I'd ever do — but at the end I knew exactly where we stood financially, and would show it to him the next day for comments.

At sunset, we walked the beach, to see what havoc the hurricane had wrought

Talbot Mundy at work in Florida study.

The wind still blew strong, and the gorges cut in the sand by the pounding surf were full of debris. There was a cleansing quality in the wind, which blew the cobwebs away.

We had an invitation to a party at the Blassingames' that evening.

"Are you too tired? I can phone — "

"No. I feel swell now. Let's go."

It was a thoroughly enjoyable evening among friends, and returning home late, we stood looking up at the sky where an occasional star was visible.

He took my hand. "Let's walk to the beach once more. It's been a good day. I feel so much better than I did this morning — it's like riding an upward spiral. Tomorrow — we'll decide on that vacation. . . ."

GHOSTS WALK . . .

by Darrel Crombie

Ghosts walk when I open a book by Talbot Mundy.

I remember: a summer night; thunderous rain on taut canvas; a leaking Bell tent; seven Boy Scouts half-sitting, half-lying on piled duffel around the center pole; mosquitoes; the eye-smart from a tiny smudge-fire of birch bark; a bean-can hurricane lantern with a stub of candle; a dog-eared magazine; and a voice reading:

> "That night it rained. The wind blew yelling squalls along the streets. At intervals the din of hail on cobblestones and roofs became a stinging sea of sound."

Mundy stalwarts will recognize "The Falling Star," final chapter.

We had found the magazine (the October 23, 1926 issue of *Adventure)* on a high shelf, dust layered, during our patrol's tour of cookhouse duty the previous day. Our Patrol Leader — as befitted leadership — then commandeered the *Adventure.* Despite the evening's overcast he was well into the story of Commodus when we dropped and anchored our tent wall, and — as a precaution against a sudden shower — let out the guy ropes. (For the uninitiated: canvas that is not waterproofed shrinks when it gets wet . . . and can pull out tent pegs.)

Rain came; a savage downpour.

We awoke to darkness, sound, water: water dripping from the bell slope, water crawling inward beneath the tent wall. Everything was damp or sodden; and mosquito song was a high thin endless accompaniment to drumming rain.

By the time we located our Edgeworth tin of head-waxed matches; lit the candle stub in the lantern; coaxed birch bark into unwilling smoulder; and arranged our gear around the center post; we were wide-awake, restless, uncomfortable. (Next morning we learned two Patrols had forgotten to let out their guy ropes — but those tents were on a distant side of the field; so *we* had no visitors.)

One bright Scout (killed at Caen during World War Two) suggested that since there was only one light, one copy of *Adventure,* our Patrol Leader should sketch-in the story of Commodus, then read aloud from the point he had earlier left off.

> "The wavering oil lanterns died out one by one and left the streets in darkness in which now and then a slave-borne litter laboured like a boat caught spreading too much sail. The overloaded sewers backed up and made pools of foulness, difficult to ford. Along the Tiber banks there was panic . . . "

"The Falling Star," final chapter.
That was my introduction to the writing of Talbot Mundy.

           *   *   *   *   *   *   *   *

At that point in time, *Adventure* filled a need. In broader scope, that was the success secret of the mass-market magazines: each filled a need. Unlike the "slicks," which were advertising showcases, the "pulps" supplied solid pages of plot, formula, fast-action: unabashed escapism.

Needed escapism.

Living, in the Twenties, was neither cushioned nor plastic-wrapped.

Electricity (for those within reach of power poles, or who could afford it) supplied *lighting* for the home. Refrigeration depended on ice: neat blocks dropped into a top compartment of the ice-box from tongs of the Ice Man. Coal and wood (cities could boast gas mains) fired the kitchen stove: the integral source of heat for cooking, baking, and the range-boiler that supplied household hot-water . . . and a kitchen stove demanded continuous fueling and maintenance the year around; furnaces, too, were hand-stoked with coal. Always, there was the added chore of soot and ash removal.

A telephone was a luxury; radio, in its infancy; TV, a future dream. Silent movies struggled to become "talkies."

But postal service was speedy and reliable.

Trains and ships (both dependent upon hand-fired coal) combined to bring the outpourings of the world's presses with daily regularity to the newsstands (perhaps twice a year British mail would arrive a day late because of a storm at sea); . . . and magazines were dated for the week in which they arrived.

That regularity, a stability of resource, created habit; and gave fiction new impetus, new status.

Friends and acquaintances were categorized by the fiction they read.

In our neighborhood of gardens, lawns, and tree-shaded streets, homes were mostly of professional people: a doctor, a dentist, a civil engineer, a high school teacher, two steel plant foremen, a newspaper publisher. My father was a mine official and Justice of the Peace; my mother, a school teacher.

The neighborhood's eight girls, twelve boys, shared magazines: an amalgam which included *Adventure, Argosy/All-Story, Weird Tales, Detective Fiction Weekly, Blue Book, Union Jack, Sexton Blake Library,* and *Chums.*

Each magazine captured a different mood.

In *Adventure,* first read was "The Camp-Fire" — a wondrous fellowship of sharing between editor, author, and reader. Arthur Sullivant Hoffman, inaugurator of "The Camp-Fire," was, of course, the canny editor who early established *Adventure* as top rank in the straightforward adventure field. (What Hoffman expected from his writers is well laid down in his book: FUNDA-MENTALS OF FICTION WRITING, published by The Bobbs-Merrill Company in 1922.)

No false note jarred. The reader was kept in the illusion.

Talbot Mundy was adept at building and maintaining an illusion. In his tales, whether of the East or the conquests and intrigues of Ancient Rome, there is always an underlying theme of man-in-search-of-himself: the Ancient Wisdom. On occasion, the Empire of Rudyard Kipling lingers (and perhaps some echoes from *The Boy's Own Paper,* which — disclaimers aside — must have been part of Mundy's boyhood). The quests are in the best H. Rider Haggard tradition.

But the overall mix, the new blend, is strictly Talbot Mundy.

An Eastern mystique.

His book titles whisper of other times and other places: TROS OF SAMO-THRACE, KING — OF THE KHYBER RIFLES, OM — THE SECRET OF AHBOR VALLEY, WINDS OF THE WORLD, GUNS OF THE GODS, THE NINE UNKNOWN, THE DEVIL'S GUARD, CAVES OF TERROR, THE LION OF PETRA. The list goes on . . .

*　　*　　*　　*　　*　　*　　*　　*

I remember: a summer night; thunderous rain on taut canvas; a leaking

Bell tent; seven Boy Scouts half-sitting, half-lying, on piled duffel around the center pole . . . and a voice reading:

> " . . . Then let me go too, or else kill me. I am no more use. This is the second time that I have failed to serve the world by tutoring a Caesar. Commodus the hero, and now you the — "
>
> "Silence!" Marcia commanded. "Or even Pertinax may rise above his scruples! Write a death certificate at once, and go your way, and follow Sextus!"

We were back in Ancient Rome. We stayed there: long after the last sentence was read . . . the rain a murmur . . . the candle a finality of black wick.

"The Falling Star," final chapter.

Ghosts walk when I open a book by Talbot Mundy.

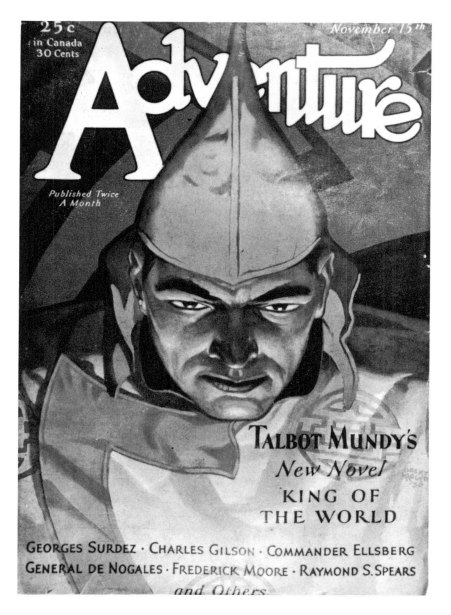

Hubert Rogers' *Adventure* magazine cover for "King of the
World." Reproduced by permission of Popular Publications, Inc. Photograph by Charles N. Brown.

TALBOT MUNDY IN *ADVENTURE*

Of all the "pulp" magazines of the 1900's, my favorite is *Adventure*. In its long history — it began in November 1910 and lasted well into the 1950's — *Adventure* cultivated a style of writing that was a notch or two above that of the average pulp. Numbered among its dependables were such writers as Harold Lamb, Arthur O. Friel, Hugh Pendexter, Arthur D. Howden Smith, Rafael Sabatini, H. Bedford-Jones, and, of course, Talbot Mundy. Indeed, the history of *Adventure* is closely tied to Talbot Mundy, and in part the magazine is a chronicle of his life.

Mundy's first contribution to *Adventure* was an article called "Pig Sticking in India," which appeared in the April 1911 issue. To the best of my knowledge, this is the second Talbot Mundy piece ever to see print — preceded only by "A Transaction in Diamonds" in the February 1911 *Scrap Book* magazine. "Pig Sticking in India" was one of four magazine appearances in *Adventure* during the year 1911. From that point — with a few noteworthy lapses — Mundy was more or less a regular contributor to the magazine until his death in 1940.

Most of Mundy's best fiction appeared in *Adventure* — including *all* of the Jimgrim stories, and *all* of the Tros episodes in which Tros was the central character — and many of his important novels including OM, THE DEVIL'S GUARD, and THE IVORY TRAIL ("On the Trail of Tippoo Tib"). More than one hundred and sixty issues carried contributions from Talbot Mundy.

The talented Arthur Sullivant Hoffman became editor shortly after the magazine's inception, remaining in charge until the late 1920's. Under his capable direction, Mundy developed and prospered, while *Adventure* grew into a bi-weekly, and for one lengthy period of the 1920's it was issued three times a month, a highly praised periodical. And in one eventful experiment of those fabulous '20's, *Adventure* made a brief attempt to become something more than a pulp — a term unpopular with some of the better writers of the day — when it published on a good quality book paper.

One of Hoffman's major contributions was a magazine department called "The Camp-Fire," which was open to author and reader alike. Its contents were fascinating reading then, and they remain so today in a world much smaller and more complex. The Camp-Fire had its inception on May 5, 1912 with the June issue of *Adventure;* it was made to order for Talbot Mundy. Thousands of words issued from his versatile pen, explaining and complementing his fiction. The high point of his Camp-Fire writings came in 1925, when Mundy took aim at recorded history's view of Julius Caesar and the Roman world. The resulting furor was unlike anything previously seen in the pulps. Mundy's opinion drew fire from many prominent readers and writers, and legions flocked to his defence as battle lines were formed. The Camp-Fire writings for 1925 are a behind-the-scenes look at the theories which allowed Mundy to write the Tros saga. The controversy that arose over these facts is a tribute to the author's enormous popularity.

This section, TALBOT MUNDY IN *ADVENTURE*, is organized chronologically. Materials are listed by month and year, and are identified with regard to length according to the magazine's designation. Appearances in The Camp-Fire are also provided. It should be noted that in earlier stories the word "novel" is used to describe what now would be termed "novella" or "novelette." This section also provides a locale or background for the story (in parenthesis), along with an identification of series characters. The following abbreviations are used:

BB = Billy Blain
CG = Chullunder Ghose
DA = Dick Anthony
JG = James Schuyler Grim (Jimgrim)
KI = Athelstan King
MO = Lord Montdidier (Monty)
MS = Meldrum Strange
OA = Fred Oakes

OH = Larry O'Hara
OM = Cottswold Ommony
QU = Ben Quorn
RA = Jeff Ramsden
RO = Jeremy Ross
TR = Tros of Samothrace
YA = Yasmini
YE = Bill Yerkes

April	*Pig Sticking in India*	Article
July	*Single-Handed Yachting*	Article
August	*The Phantom Battery* (India)	Short Story
December	*The Blooding of the Queen's Own* (Crimean War)	Short Story

Talbot Mundy's first two contributions to *Adventure* were articles of seven pages each. "The Phantom Battery," Mundy's first fiction in *Adventure,* is a six-page short story of northern India and the Sepoy Rebellion. "The Blooding of the Queen's Own" is a seven-page story of the Crimean War.

Mundy was introduced to the readers in the December 1911 issue:

> Shake hands quickly with Mr. Mundy — there is only time for me to whisper these words quickly in your ear: An Englishman — India, China, the Himalayas, Singapore, the Straits Settlements, Persian Gulf, the Boer War, Australia, Tasmania, Delagoa Bay and Lorenzo Marquez, British and German East Africa, elephant-hunting, pig-sticking, single-handed yachting, two campaigns against African tribes, sailing before the mast —

Ten years later in The Camp-Fire, September 3, 1921, editor Arthur Sullivant Hoffman admitted: "He (Talbot Mundy) told me that when he first met me he took a violent dislike to me and I confess I eyed him with doubt for a year or two."

Adventure, in its long history, was never overly concerned with illustrations, but its early issues did carry headings and decorations. Wilfred Jones produced the heading for the first Mundy effort, "Pig Sticking in India."

Other contributors appearing in *Adventure* in 1911 included: William Hope Hodgson, John Buchan, Rafael Sabatini, William Wallace Cook, Damon Runyon, Cutcliffe Hyne, Peter B. Kyne, and George Jean Nathan.

1912

January	*For Valour* (Egypt; dervishes)	Short Story
February	*The Soul of a Regiment* (Egypt; dervishes)	Short Story
	The Goner? (Boxing; BB)	Short Story
	(as Walter Galt)	
March	*The Chaplain of the Mullingars* (India)	Short Story
April	*W. Mayes — the Amazing*	Article
May	*The Queen — God Bless Her* (Crimean War)	Short Story
	Francis Bannerman — A Man of Mystery and History	Article
	(as Walter Galt)	
June	*T. C. Ansell — Adventurer*	Article
	The Second Rung (Boxing; BB)	Short Story
	(as Walter Galt)	
July	*The Cowards* (Boer War)	Short Story
	Elephant Hunting for a Living	Article
	(as Walter Galt)	
August	*The Payment of Quinn's Debt* (Africa)	Short Story
	Dorg's Luck (Boxing; BB)	Short Story
	(as Walter Galt)	
September	*In Winter Quarters* (Peninsular War)	Short Story
October	*The Man Who Saw* (India)	Short Story
	Across the Color Line (Boxing; BB)	Short Story
	(as Walter Galt)	
November	*Honor* (India)	Short Story
	Love and War (Boxing; BB)	Short Story
	(as Walter Galt)	
December	*Rabbit* (Boer War)	Short Story
	The Top of the Ladder (Boxing; BB)	Short Story
	(as Walter Galt)	

In 1912, *Adventure* carried sixteen short stories and four articles by Talbot Mundy, including the oft-reprinted "The Soul of a Regiment." In January 1912, a month before its appearance, editor Arthur Sullivant Hoffman told the *Adventure* readers: "Read it and compare it with some of Kipling's." In the February issue Hoffman added:

And Talbot Mundy has also that intangible thing called the 'story-teller's gift.' Read "The Soul of a Regiment" and decide for yourself. Maybe it will make the thrills run up and down your spine. Maybe not. They ran up and down mine when I read it, and an editorial spine is popularly supposed to be tolerably thrill-proof.

In the same issue, Hoffman noted: "Mundy fought at Colseno. . . . as a bearer of important dispatches under a terrific fire that mowed down the grass behind him as he rode. Thereby hangs a tale, but Mr. Mundy is afflicted with modesty."

The Camp-Fire, "A Meeting-Place for Readers, Writers and Adventurers," began with the June issue. One month later, Mundy was at hand in its pages to relate a remarkable tale that was told to him in Africa. In December, he was back again with a humorous anecdote of South Africa.

The Billy Blain stories, written under the pseudonym of "Walter Galt" (Mundy's father was Walter Galt Gribbon), began in the February 1912 issue. When the series ended with a final episode in February 1916, a total of ten stories had appeared.

January	*Three Helios* (Boer War)	Short Story
February	*A Low-Veldt Funeral*	Article
	One Year Later (Boxing; BB)	Short Story
	(as Walter Galt)	
March	*For the Salt Which He Had Eaten* (India)	Novelette
April	*Private Murdock's G.C.M.* (Humor, British Army)	Short Story
May	*The Guzzler's Grand Prix* (Horse Racing)	Novel
June	*At Maneuvers* (British Army)	Short Story
July	*Hookum Hai* (India, Sepoy Rebellion)	Novel
August	*The Closed Trail of William Walker*	Article
September	*The Letter of His Orders* (India)	Novel
October	*In a Righteous Cause* (India)	Novelette
November	*An Arabian Night* (Persian Gulf)	Novelette
December	*The Tempering of Harry Blunt* (India)	Novelette

Talbot Mundy continued his regular contributions to *Adventure* in 1913. "Three Helios" in the January issue was accompanied by an anecdote of the Boer War printed on the reverse of the contents page. For the first time, Mundy's tales were of more than short story length. The magazine's terminology has been used to describe the stories' length, and the three novels published in 1913 contain between 30,000 and 35,000 words each. The novelettes measure approximately 9,000 words.

In the June 1913 issue, Mundy advertised in the "Lost Trails" department of *Adventure*, seeking to learn the whereabouts of two old friends who had adventured with him in other parts of the globe.

The inside front cover of the December 1913 issue was devoted to "A Soldier and a Gentleman" — scheduled for the January 1914 issue:

> You'll lose your heart to Yasmini, the brown-eyed Hindoo maid, who is the heroine of this exciting romance. All India knew the mysterious Yasmini and her golden beauty, but not a soul knew where she came from. They sang songs of the lure in her eyes from Peshawur to Cape Cormorin, and the jingle of her anklets, as she danced, was music to the ears of many. An Anglo-Indian soldier, a native Maharaja

and a dastardly dacoit who dared to lift his shifty eyes up to Yasmini, figure in this adventurous story of love and action. The rich color of the Orient makes a fitting background for the swiftly moving scenes. You will never regret following Yasmini's fortunes. There are many other rattling good shorter stories in the 224 pages of this January (1914) issue.

January	*A Soldier and a Gentleman* (India; YA)	Novelette
February	*For the Peace of India* (India)	Serial, Part 1 of 3
March	*For the Peace of India*	Serial, Part 2 of 3
April	*For the Peace of India*	Serial, Part 3 of 3
June	*The Gentility of Ikey Blumendall* (British Army)	Short Story
July	*Gulbaz and the Game* (India, Secret Service)	Novelette
August	*Dick Anthony of Arran: The Sword of Iskander* (Scotland-Egypt; DA)	Novelette
September	*Foul of the Czar* (Near East; DA)	Novelette
	Nothing Doing (Western) (as Walter Galt)	Short Story
October	*"Go, Tell the Czar!"* (Persia; DA)	Novelette
November	*King Dick* (Persia; DA)	Novelette
December	*The Lancing of the Whale* (Persia; DA)	Novelette

In the January issue, "A Soldier and a Gentleman" introduced Yasmini, the vivacious Eurasian girl who is a major figure in Mundy's famous KING — OF THE KHYBER RIFLES, as well as in other tales. A month later in The Camp-Fire, Mundy accompanied the first installment of his serial with information on the Rajputs.

In the May issue of *Adventure,* in the department "The Trail Ahead," the editor provided some further information:

> Talbot Mundy is one of the half-dozen best storytellers in the United States. And I think you'll say it with me. Our recent serial was his first, but it was seized upon months before for book publication by Scribner's in this country and Cassell's in England. And he's been writing only about two years!

The serial mentioned by Hoffman was "For the Peace of India," which was printed in book form as RUNG HO!

In the July issue, Hoffman established in The Camp-Fire that Mundy was now living in Maine:

Hugh Pendexter and Talbot Mundy both live in the same little town in Maine. Consequently said town has two novelettes to its credit in this issue of the magazine. I take particular interest in this fact because I introduced Mr. Mundy to both Maine and Mr. Pendexter. Talbot Mundy has been pretty well over Europe, Asia, Africa, and Australia. He is English, as you know. Last Summer he joined me in camp in Maine. He arrived after dark. In the morning he took one long breath of Maine air, one long look at a Maine lake and Maine woods, and announced: "This is God's country! I'm going to live here!"

A few days later, at our earnest solicitation, Hugh Pendexter came up from the coast where he was spending the Summer and dropped in for the night. Once a newspaperman in New York, he too, had been won to Maine, and I knew he was familiar with the whole State and could give valuable information as to the very best part of it to settle in. The three of us sat around the fire that night and he proceeded to prove that he had himself settled down in the very best spot in all Maine. Talbot Mundy has now been living in that spot for the better part of a year.

It was up there that *Dick Anthony of Arran* was born. Who is *Dick Anthony of Arran?* All of you are going to meet him next month. He is *the* adventurer. Stow his name away in your mind — *Dick Anthony of Arran*. Talbot Mundy has written a series of stories about him, and the first of them appears in the next issue.

The Dick Anthony stories were tales of a Scots adventurer fighting against Russia. There were eight tales in the series, completing in the March 1915 issue.

The town in Maine where Mundy settled was Norway, northwest of Portland and not far from the New Hampshire border. Hugh Pendexter, a prolific contributor to *Adventure* and a widely published author in his own right, lived here until his death in 1940 — also the year of Mundy's death.

In the August issue of *Adventure,* Arthur Sullivant Hoffman wrote more about Mundy's techniques:

Talbot Mundy is one of the fastest writers I know. Some of his stories have come to us in the very first draft, just as he wrote them off on the typewriter, *and* his "copy" is always about as "clean" as an editor gets. Sometimes he has written a story, destroyed it entire, written it all over again, destroyed the second copy, and so on for, maybe, three or four times, but each time the writing is done quickly, smoothly, and in finished form.

In this issue you have the first story of *Dick Anthony of Arran*, "The Sword of Iskander," a complete novelette, the beginning of a series giving the adventures of this same *Dick Anthony*, who moves on to bigger and bigger deeds, concerning which I will not tell you one single word in advance. Except this. On *this* story Talbot Mundy has *not* worked quickly. He could have done a long serial in the same time and with half the work.

This time he set out to do something stronger and bigger than he had ever done before. Plot after plot was discarded. Time and again he put on his skis — you will remember that now he lives in a little town in the Maine woods — and went out alone for a day in the open, where little ideas fall away and you find big ones in their place. Snow and the pine-trees, lake, river, and the everlasting hills by day, the flames of a roaring fire on his own hearth by night; every minute and every faculty were strained to the utmost in pursuit of the one big conception that would bring him the man and the deeds he must have to make this story what he had set his heart on making it. And he found them.

Then came the writing of it. Write and destroy, write and destroy, write and destroy. The words must be equal to the theme. Write and destroy, and go on writing. *Dick Anthony* was a living being by this time and his deeds had become an epic. With a tale like that to tell, could he let it be merely a good story instead of the throbbing, pulsing reality it was to him?

And at last it was done.

It came to me just as the office day was closing. I began to read it. Long after the others had all gone home I sat alone and read it to the end. Perhaps it would be nearer the mark to say I lived it. And now it is your turn to meet *Dick Anthony of Arran.*

January	*Disowned!* (Persia; DA)	Novelette
February	*No Name!* (Persia; DA)	Novelette
March	*On Terms* (Persia; DA)	Novelette
April	*MacHassan Ah* (British sailors, Arabia)	Novelette
May	*A Temporary Trade in Titles* (Humor)	Short Story
June	*The Dove With a Broken Wing* (India)	Short Story
July	*The Winds of the World* (India; YA)	Serial, Part 1 of 3
August	*The Winds of the World*	Serial, Part 2 of 3
September	*The Winds of the World*	Serial, Part 3 of 3
November	*The Return of Billy Blain* (Boxing; BB) (as Walter Galt)	Short Story

The March issue of *Adventure* carried a drawing of Talbot Mundy on the inside front cover, a rather severe man with glasses and mustache. The July Camp-Fire made a brief mention of Hoffman's earlier meeting with Hugh Pendexter in Maine, in company with Mundy.

The Camp-Fire in the September issue contained an untitled poem which Hoffman described: "Without any warning whatsoever Talbot Mundy sent me the following poem, of which I am the hero — if you want to call it that."

'E DEKKOS at yer sideways, and there's murder in his glim—
    Oh my-y-y! Oh my!
And a brace o' clerks are seatin' wet, a' tremblin', watchin' him
    A-opening his briefs—Oh, my!
He grips a bloody Dyak kris, and jams it in a chit,
An' rips the paper open like a feller's throat was slit;
An' 'e lets a 'tween-deck whisper, an' the two clerks throws a fit,
'Cause 'e likes to see 'em gurgulin'—Oh, my-y-y!
And it's always best to humor 'im—Oh, my!

HE SITS an' chews his fingers while 'e reads his mornin' mail—
    Oh, say-ay-ay! Oh, say!
And his roving eye gets haggard, and his livid lips are pale—
    For the things 'e reads! Oh, say!

And the tiger-skin 'e sits on, and the python on the floor;
And the awful, hugly devil-fish what hangs above the door;
An' the juju, an' the fetish, an' the boot what J. James wore,
They tremle 'cause 'e shudders so—Oh, say-ay-ay!
An' the clerks—Oh, watch 'em shudder too! Oh, say!

THERE'S a Chinese stink-pot handy on the desk beside the ink—
Oh, Gee-ee-ee! Oh, Gee!
An' 'e'll use it on yer lively, yes, an' sooner than yer'd think,
If yer didn't beat it quick—Oh Gee!
He drinks hot blood for breakfast, an' he likes it in a pail,
And 'e spends his off-hours watchin' for the black flag on the jail;
And you mustn't never go and tie no crackers to his tail—
Oh, Hully Gee! Oh, Gee!
Because he's got rejection-slips he'd send yer through the mail—
Oh, Gee!

TM

January	*Billy Blain Eats Biscuits* (Boxing; BB) (as Walter Galt)	Short Story
February	*A Drop or Two of White* (India)	Short Story
	Billy Blain's Onions and Garlic (Boxing; BB) (as Walter Galt)	Short Story
	Tucker's Tongue	Article

The final Billy Blain stories by "Walter Galt" appeared in the January and February 1916 issues. Mundy's output in *Adventure* during that year was significantly low — and for good reason. The May and June issues carried full page advertisements for "King, of the Khyber Rifles" on the inside front cover. The story began in the May issue of *Everybody's Magazine,* and it was Mundy's longest and most fantastic fiction to date, spread out over nine issues, and lasting until January 1917. *Everybody's* was another publication of the Ridgway Company — a companion magazine to *Adventure.* But unlike *Adventure, Everybody's* welcomed illustration, and "King, of the Khyber Rifles" was accompanied by more than 100 designs, devices and illustrations from the master American penman, Joseph Clement Coll. The result is an incredible effort; one of those rare, perfect marriages of art and fiction.

1917

April	*The Soul of a Regiment* (Egypt; dervishes)	Short Story
May	*The Damned Old Nigger* (Africa)	Short Story
Mid-October	*Hira Singh's Tale* (World War I, Sikhs)	Serial, Part 1 of 4
First November	*Hira Singh's Tale*	Serial, Part 2 of 4
Mid-November	*Hira Singh's Tale*	Serial, Part 3 of 4
First December	*Hira Singh's Tale*	Serial, Part 4 of 4

The February Camp-Fire announced that "The Soul of a Regiment" would be reprinted in April — the first story in *Adventure's* history to be so treated. Hoffman called it "a perfect specimen of its type," and in the July issue quoted a reader: "I don't mind saying I cried over the end of Talbot Mundy's 'The Soul of a Regiment.'" Its sequel, "The Damned Old Nigger," appeared in the May issue.

In September, *Adventure* increased its publication schedule to twice-a-month, and Hoffman reported that Talbot Mundy had recently become an American citizen. A month later, in the Mid-October Camp-Fire, Hoffman prefaced the appearance of "Hira Singh's Tale" with some information on Mundy's writing habits and activities:

> I am glad to add that Talbot Mundy not so long ago became an American citizen, I being one of his two witnesses required by law. I wish our country could gain many more citizens like him. He is chairman of the agricultural committee of his county down in Maine and I understand that that county leads the State and most of New England in its practical accomplishment for war-relief production and conservation of crops.

Mid-August	*"Blighty"*	Article
First December	*Oakes Respects an Adversary* (Africa; OA, MO)	Novelette

"Blighty" from the Mid-August issue is a brief article providing the derivation of the word. The First December issue introduced a new series and carried the subtitle: "An Up and Down the Earth Tale." "Oakes Respects an Adversary" is a novelette of Portuguese East Africa and the adventurers Bill Oakes and Lord Montdidier. In The Camp-Fire for the First December issue Mundy provided 750 words of background, from which the following is quoted:

> This, and the stories that will follow, are all more or less reminiscent. The names of people have been so entirely changed that the originals are unrecognizable, except that the man Charles du Maurier under his real name made such a reputation on that countryside as to be undisguisable anyhow. Any one who lived in Lourenço Marques in the bad old days of monarchial government would need no spirit of divination to help him identify the original of du Maurier and his family, even if I had called him Jones.

By a wide margin, voting by readers proclaimed "The Soul of a Regiment" the most popular short story to appear in *Adventure* during 1917. "The Damned Old Nigger" was a strong third in the same category, while "Hira Singh's Tale" finished in third place in the novel category, not far from the first place selection.

1919

First January	*America Horns In* (Africa; OA, MO, YE)	Novelette
February 18	*Jackson Tactics* (Africa; OA, MO, YE)	Novelette
Mid-March	*Heinie Horns into the Game* (Africa; OA, MO, YE)	
		Novelette
First May	*On the Trail of Tippoo Tib* (Africa; OA, MO, YE)	
		Serial, Part 1 of 6
Mid-May	*On the Trail of Tippoo Tib*	Serial, Part 2 of 6
First June	*On the Trail of Tippoo Tib*	Serial, Part 3 of 6
Mid-June	*On the Trail of Tippoo Tib*	Serial, Part 4 of 6
First July	*On the Trail of Tippoo Tib*	Serial, Part 5 of 6
Mid-July	*On the Trail of Tippoo Tib*	Serial, Part 6 of 6
First September	*The Shriek of Dûm* (Red Sea; OA, MO, YE)	Novelette
Mid-September	*Some Sayings of "Hell-Fire" Smith*	Article
Mid-October	*Barabbas Island* (Egypt; OA, MO, YE)	Novel

The "Up and Down the Earth Tales" which had begun in December 1918 continued throughout 1919. Oakes and Lord Montdidier were quickly joined by an American, Will Yerkes, adventuring through seven episodes that year. They included the novel, "Barabbas Island," and the long serial, "On the Trail of Tippoo Tib," which was published in book form by the Bobbs-Merrill Company as THE IVORY TRAIL. It remains one of Mundy's best known tales.

In the February 18 Camp-Fire, Hoffman wrote:

> When I first read Talbot Mundy's "Up and Down the Earth Tales" I wrote him that I didn't like *Monty,* that he got on my nerves just as he got on the nerves of *Yerkes* the American, and couldn't he tone *Monty* down a bit? I figured *Monty* would rile other democratic Americans as he had *Yerkes* and me.

In a reply of close to 500 words, partially quoted here, Mundy responded:

Don't consider my feelings; I simply haven't any left after reading what you say about my friend *Monty*.

        *   *   *   *   *

See here — from first to last I have never pretended *Monty* is a democrat. I don't pretend he's right. He's a character; and the proof he is one lies in the fact that you hate him. You wouldn't hate a nonentity, would you?

        *   *   *   *   *

Monty is the type of man who led the men who died in Flanders. Under the mellowing influence of *Yerkes* I rather expect he will undergo a lot of transmogrification, if that's the proper word.

        *   *   *   *   *

You ask me to think it over. Gosh! Did I do no thinking before I took out final papers? I'm an American from choice, because I'm convinced that this America of ours begins to think at about the point where the rest of the world leaves off.

In the First April 1919 Camp-Fire, Talbot Mundy contributed a 5,000-word autobiography which is reproduced in entirety elsewhere in this volume. The First July Camp-Fire provided the readers' preferences for 1918. Mundy's only fiction of that year, "Oakes Respects an Adversary," placed eighth in popularity among stories of less than 20,000 words.

Mid-January   *In Aleppo Bazaar* (Near East; OA, MO, YE)   Novel

"In Aleppo Bazaar" in the Mid-January issue was the final "Up and Down the Earth Tale" to appear in *Adventure*. It was the only Mundy story to appear in the magazine during that year. However, a final tale of the adventurers Oakes, Montdidier and Yerkes — "The Eye of Zeitun" (published in book form as THE EYE OF ZEITOON) — appeared in a companion magazine, *Romance*, in the same year.

In the First July issue, reader voting established "On the Trail of Tippoo Tib" and "The Shriek of Dûm" as fifth and sixth in popularity among tales published in 1919.

March 3	*Guns of the Gods* (India; YA)	Serial, Part 1 of 5
March 18	*Guns of the Gods*	Serial, Part 2 of 5
April 3	*Guns of the Gods*	Serial, Part 3 of 5
April 18	*Guns of the Gods*	Serial, Part 4 of 5
May 3	*Guns of the Gods*	Serial, Part 5 of 5
November 10	*The Adventure at El Kerak* (Near-East; JG)	Novel
December 10	*Under the Dome of the Rock* (Near-East; JG)	Novel

In 1921, Yasmini — who was first introduced to *Adventure* readers in "A Soldier and a Gentleman" in 1914 — appeared in the long serial, "Guns of the Gods." This is a tale of Yasmini's youth, and Mundy's original title for it was "In the Days of Her Youth." In The Camp-Fire for July 18, editor Arthur Sullivant Hoffman quoted from a Mundy letter: "No, she's not an historical character. I once saw a vision of an Indian lady in Bombay through the open door of a shattered carriage. She smiled at me, and *Yasmini* was born that minute."

On his own, Hoffman admitted: "He didn't write that for publication but I'm taking a chance. Which shows great courage on my part, for Talbot Mundy is over six feet, a very husky person and with every right in the world to resent any fool inference that he is a lady-killer."

Later in the year (September 3) Hoffman added:

> He (Talbot Mundy) told me that when he first met me he took a violent dislike to me and I confess I eyed him with doubt for a year or two. Finally we camped together in Maine, two of us, and that settled it. I remember Hugh Pendexter came over from Norway (Maine) some sixty miles distant just out of the kindness of his heart to give us more dope on this Maine Mundy and I were so crazy about, sat on his heels at our fire one night and was gone early in the morning.

In the January 18 issue of *Adventure*, Hoffman reported that Mundy "is just recently back from most of a year in Palestine and Arabia, and that locality just now is about as good a place for real adventures as any one could ask for." In the March 10 issue, Hoffman revealed that Mundy had completed the first two novelettes in a new series for *Adventure* "laid in this exceedingly turbulent and interesting section of the globe." Before the end of the year, the two had appeared. "The Adventure at El Kerak" and "Under the Dome of the Rock" served to introduce one of Mundy's greatest heroes, and certainly his most prolific one. He was, of course, "Jimgrim" — James Schuyler Grim, an American drawn from life who carried a commission in the British army "without giving up his American citizenship or at least lying about it." In the second episode, "Under the Dome of the Rock," the Sikh, Narayan Singh, is introduced. As yet, however, the broad cast of characters who will be associated with Grim in his long career have not surfaced.

In the December 10 issue, Mundy contributed the following to The Camp-Fire:

> The chief difficulty about these *Jimgrim* stories has been to hide "Grim's" real identity. I believe he was the first American ever commissioned in the British Army without going through the farce of pretending to be a Canadian; he stuck out for his citizenship, and, as they wanted him badly, he had his way.
>
> Colonel Lawrence is probably the only man in the world who knows the Arab better than "Grim" does; he fought behind Lawrence all through that wonderful campaign on Allenby's right wing, doing the unseen, unsung spade-work. Now that the war is over they have kept "Grim" on the staff for what is known as "special duty," and he goes pretty well where he likes.
>
> His methods are quite peculiar. He makes friends where he likes, in the jail or out of it; a man's crimes seem to make no difference to him; he isn't concerned about other folks' morals, but takes men and women as he finds them. And he possesses a perfect genius for stalling trouble by hunting for the high spots of human character. One favorite trick of his is to use small boys as spies — the smaller the better; sometimes they realize they are being so used, and oftener not.

Narayan Singh, like "Grim," is a personal friend of mine. He is one of those born soldiers who never gets promoted, for the reason that about once in six months he takes an awful lot too much whisky, and, when primed, not even his beloved British colonel can make him behave. In between times he is one of those rare men whose friendship makes you stand straight. I never could draw a color line. I hate a mean white much more than I do the vilest negro, for it seems obvious to me that the mean white has had a chance to know better, whereas the negro hasn't. Of course, there is nothing negroish about a Sikh, but there are folk who object to them on racial grounds. Lacking that racial prejudice, I found it much less difficult than most men do to get on terms with "Grim," who, as I said, makes friends "wherever he darned well chooses." He sticks to his friends, too, and they stand by him, as will transpire in future stories.

In October of 1921, under the guiding hand of Arthur Sullivant Hoffman, *Adventure* went to a publication of three issues a month. Perhaps this was due in part to the promise of additional tales from Talbot Mundy, and in the succeeding months there came a heavy output from the pen of that talented author. Mundy was coming into his own.

January 10	*The "Iblis" at Lud* (Near-East; JG)	Novel
February 20	*The Seventeen Thieves of El-Kalil* (Near-East; JG)	Novel
March 20	*The Lion of Petra* (Near-East; JG)	Novel
April 20	*The Woman Ayisha* (Near-East; JG)	Novel
May 30	*The Lost Trooper* (Near-East; JG, RO)	Novel
July 10	*The King in Check* (Near-East; JG, RO, RA)	Novel
August 10	*A Secret Society* (Egypt; JG, RA, RO, MS)	Novel
September 10	*Moses and Mrs. Aintree* (Egypt; JG, RA, RO, MS)	Novel
October 10	*Khufu's Real Tomb* (Egypt; JG, RA, MS)	Novel
November 10	*The Gray Mahatma* (India; RA, KI, YA)	Novel
December 10	*Benefit of Doubt* (India; OM, KI)	Novel

In the year 1922, *Adventure* was published a total of thirty-six times, and Talbot Mundy's fiction was represented in eleven issues with close to a half million words. In addition, there are several thousands words of explanation, theory, and response to readers' queries in The Camp-Fire. In 1922 there was a new confidence, a new audacity about his writings, as Mundy molded a pantheon of heroes in situations which were becoming increasingly more mystic.

More about Grim appeared in the March 20 Camp-Fire:

> The original of Grim — and he is an American, and very much alive — has the peculiar and highly developed gift of passing himself for an Arab. He has actually made the pilgrimage to Mecca more than once — on one occasion overland, and once by train. I only hope I have disguised his identity sufficiently to satisfy his strict injunctions on that point. He is not a good talker about himself, but he has promised to give me the "makings" of a lot more yarns "some day," subject to that one proviso, that I give no clue to his real name.

In the first six "Jimgrim" episodes, Grim was assisted by the Sikh, Narayan Singh, and by an unnamed narrator — finally identified in "The King in Check" as Jeff Ramsden. In the seventh episode, Mundy introduced the outspoken Australian, Jeremy Ross, a veteran of the Boer War.

In "The King in Check," Jimgrim was determined to establish Feisul, third son of the King of Mecca, as king of the Arabs. Editor Arthur Sullivant Hoffman informed the readers "that Mr. Mundy has in these *Jimgrim* stories set forth faithfully a very remarkable knowledge of the inside of things that have been happening in Palestine and Arabia these past few years." Mundy himself furnished the following report:

> The description of Feisul is drawn at first hand. He is like good wine that needs no bush; you can't say enough in his praise, or overdraw the man's impressive manliness, any more than you can overstate the meanness of the method used to get rid of him.

> I refuse to say how much of this story is true. Treat it as fiction, and let it go at that; it happens to amuse me to take drab facts and weave a story out of them, and I don't know that they're worse material than whole-cloth inventions would be. But if you're still curious, I'll admit this: I was in Damascus while Feisul was playing that loosing hand, and I had the whole story from his own lips of the Arab share in the great war, of the Allies' promises, and of how they had been broken after the armistice, when Arab friendship didn't look quite so necessary as it did when the promises were given. We talked for hours, but he never once complained on his own account. He is an Arab patriot first and last, with no other aim than to see his nation self-determined and ruled by a government of their own choosing.

With the August 10 publication of "A Secret Society," Mundy moved to new horizons. Grim was persuaded to leave his commission in the British army by Ross and Ramsden, and the three formed a business triumpherate, with Narayan Singh assisting. At this point, Mundy introduced Meldrum Strange, one of the "nine richest men in the world," who employed the trio in an endeavor against international criminals. In a Camp-Fire observation of August 10, Mundy elaborated:

Meldrum Strange is an attempt to draw the composite of three men, two of whom I knew personally, one of whom gave me permission to use him in a story if I liked, and one of whom I only saw, heard speak and admired across a dinner table. All three men are multi-millionaires, and as it happens, all three of them are devoted to the thankless task of "doing some good in the world."

More interesting comment about Narayan Singh in the same Camp-Fire.

Narayan Singh, as I have said before, is a friend of mine. I received a letter from him from India this morning, in which he says he "prays daily that full madness may descend on all the politicians, so that their inflictions and abominations may increase to the point where men rebel at last, and act like men, and slay the devils." Narayan Singh rather believes in slaying as an antidote for most things. He is a magnificent swordsman, and his feat of killing in the story ("A Secret Society") is no more remarkable than the stunt he really did during the war in Palestine, for which he was called out from the ranks by a full general to be complimented and cited for decoration. He was decorated by the French as well as by the British, but thinks more of the notches in his saber than of his medals. A truculent, incredulous, amazing man, of peculiar tact at times, and of cast-iron friendship always.

When Athelstan King appeared in "The Gray Mahatma" and "Benefit of Doubt" in late 1922, he was well known to many of *Adventure's* readers. King had been introduced some six years earlier in *Adventure's* companion magazine, *Everybody's,* in the imaginative and heroic serial, "King, of the Khyber Rifles."

There is a wealth of other revealing Talbot Mundy material in the 1922 pages of the Camp-Fire. Among the most interesting is a 2,000-word contribution to the April 30 issue, partially quoted here. Mundy related:

Very briefly, the fact is that the Anglo-Saxon people are the descendants of the lost Ten Tribes of Israel. The Jews are the descendants of the Tribe of Judah only, with part of the Tribe of Levi and possibly some of Benjamin. The Ten Tribes were carried off into captivity by Tiglath-Pileser, the King of Assyria, somewhere about 800 B.C., and there is ample evidence to show that they migrated northward and spread all over Europe, gradually working their way toward those "Islands of the Sea" of which Isaiah speaks, and which were certainly the British Isles. They became established in Sweden, Norway, Scotland, Britain and the north of Ireland as the Anglo-Saxons, and the very word British is derived from the Hebrew Brith, meaning covenant. "British" means "the People of the Covenant," which in turn is a Biblical synonym for the Children of Israel.

1500 words of additional information concerning the lost tribes can be found in the September 10 Camp-Fire, while the October 10 issue, which contained the Mundy story, "Khufu's Real Tomb," discussed the great pyramid.

1923

January 10	*Treason* (India, OM)	Novel
March 20	*The Nine Unknown* (India; JG, RA, RO, KI, CG)	Serial, Part 1 of 5
March 30	*The Nine Unknown*	Serial, Part 2 of 5
April 10	*The Nine Unknown*	Serial, Part 3 of 5
April 20	*The Nine Unknown*	Serial, Part 4 of 5
April 30	*The Nine Unknown*	Serial, Part 5 of 5
August 10	*Diana Against Ephesians* (India; OM)	Novel
October 10	*The Marriage of Meldrum Strange* (India; OM, MS, RA, CG)	Novel
December 10	*Mohammed's Tooth* (India; KI, JG, RA)	Novel

In reference to "Treason" in the January 10 issue, Talbot Mundy wrote in the Camp-Fire:

> This story, the second I have placed in Moplah country with Cottswold Ommony playing alternately first and second fiddle, was designed to illustrate the dilemna, more or less, in which a decent Englishman might find himself who sympathized in his heart with Indian asperations toward self-government, yet naturally could not, would not, should not turn against his own crown.
>
> Cottswold Ommony is drawn from life. I think he is really a composite of two men I have known rather intimately — one an American in public service, faced with the ever-lasting greed of politicians, just as Ommony in the story is faced by the fangs of officialdom.
>
> Ommony is something of a pacifist, but not quite.

In the February 20 issue, Arthur Sullivant Hoffman defended Mundy in The Camp-Fire against one who accused him of British propaganda. In his defense, Hoffman noted that Mundy had also been accused of anti-British sentiment.

"The Nine Unknown," which began in the March 20 issue, was a long fantasy in which Jimgrim and his associates encountered strange mysteries of the East. It was a portend of what was to come.

Once a year, Adventure asked its readers to vote for their favorite stories. In the category "novel" as used by *Adventure*, Mundy's "The Gray Mahatma" was the top vote-getter, and "Khufu's Real Tomb" and "The Lost Trooper" placed third and fourth respectively. It should be noted, however, that the serial category produced two more popular tales in terms of total votes. They were "The Sea Hawk" by Rafael Sabatini and "Tiger River" by Arthur O. Friel. Both tales were considerably longer — double the length of the Mundy tales — and more properly what we consider "novel" length today.

In the April 30 issue, The Camp-Fire printed a long letter disagreeing with some of Mundy's statements about the Great Pyramid. Mundy replied from San Diego, California, and put forth a number of Egyptian theories in a letter of close to 2,000 words.

There was more controversy in the May 30 issue. George Castor Martin contributed a long discourse, complete with charts, on the subject of the lost tribes, the Lia Fail, and the settlement of Ireland. Mundy's response of 1200 words was printed in the same issue, in which he stated:

> Your account of the settlement of Ireland by various peoples
> is far from complete, if the authors on whom I depended
> when outlining the Ten Tribes theory are accurate. According to them the Isles of the Sea referred to in Isaiah are undoubtedly the British Isles. The tribe of Dan was a sea-faring
> race whose ships used to visit the British Isles regularly long
> before Jeremiah took the Prince of Judah to Ireland along
> with the Ark and the Lia Fail.

Writing about "Diana Against Ephesians," Mundy stated: "The story is placed in an imaginary native state on the southeast coast of India, not so far, we'll say, from Travancore, where all the oldest customs still survive." The "Diana of the title referred to Ommony's great wolfhound, and Mundy had the following to say about Cotswold Ommony:

I like Ommony. That isn't his name, of course. I met him years ago in Bengal, and he let me shoot a tiger in a forest he was managing. The tales he told at night in his little bungalow surrounded by the forest that he loves more than anything else on earth, were the most absorbing I ever heard. He is something of an astronomer, knows animals and trees as some men know arithmetic, and dreaded, as I remember, only one thing — retirement to London on a miserable pension. Funnily enough, he had a notion that the only place for a pensioned man was within a half-mile radius of Piccadilly Circus. A small flat on Shaftesbury Avenue, I think, was his idea of the inevitable. I hope he missed it!

He believed in reincarnation, although not of men's souls into the bodies of animals. He used to say it was ridiculous to suppose that sixty or seventy years could teach a man much; and equally ridiculous to imagine that the Universe could have any use for a blackguard or a fool. . . .

The natives who worked for him used to regard him as little less than a deity. I sincerely hope he isn't rotting into old age in a Shaftesbury Avenue two-room flat!

In the August 20 Camp-Fire, one of the "Ask Adventure" staff wrote of his curiosity about the conditions in German East Africa as outlined by Mundy in "On the Trail of Tippoo Tib" (THE IVORY TRAIL). His investigations led him to agreement with Mundy's position.

Millionaire Meldrum Strange returned in the October 10 issue, and Mundy had the following to say:

Having grown a little tired of always seeing the hero of a story win hands down, and reason confirming record that no hero can be found without some human weaknesses, I have trusted the reader to be patient while the hero, Ommony, sustains a rather sharp defeat — although poetic justice deals fairly by him in the end.

Another thing: I'm sore with the theory that rich men must always get the worst end. They don't in real life. So I've invited you to dislike Meldrum Strange as heartily as you see fit, but to concede him elements of manliness, even as Ommony has his streak of venom. The weight of Meldrum's moneybags is too enormous for him to have emerged anything but a winner, at least to some extent.

Chullunder Ghose is a bad, fat rascal, but I like him. Selmira Poulakis has appeared before in "A Secret Society" and it seemed unfair to leave her in the horrible predicament she was in when that story closed. As Lady Molyneau she may rise like the Phoenix from the ashes of an awkward past. Kate Ommony is new. The Ommony I used to know in real life had no sister, but he should have.

The November 30 Camp-Fire included a tongue-in-cheek letter from writer H. Bedford-Jones about the lost tribes of Israel.

October 10	*Om* (Tibet-India; OM)	Serial, Part 1 of 6
October 20	*Om*	Serial, Part 2 of 6
October 30	*Om*	Serial, Part 3 of 6
November 10	*Om*	Serial, Part 4 of 6
November 20	*Om*	Serial, Part 5 of 6
November 30	*Om*	Serial, Part 6 of 6

1924 was a sparse year for Talbot Mundy in *Adventure*. Mundy's sole contribution for the entire year was "Om," a six-part serial that involved unknown lands between Tibet and India. Still, "Om" is one of Mundy's masterpieces, and the author considered it among his best efforts. Personal correspondence reveals that early, working titles included "The Crystal Jade" and "The Ringding Gelong Lama" (which Hoffman considered too humorous), and that the author fully expected magazine rejection.

> I go on record here and now, that it is a marvel that Hoffman bought the story. It breaks all *Adventure's* rules, including, as it does, a spiritual theme and a naked white woman in the last chapter. It gets by Hoffman, and can consequently get by any criticism in the world! verb. sap.

In the October 10 issue, Arthur Sullivant Hoffman advises that opinions in "Om" are Mundy's, and not those of *Adventure*. In the same issue, Mundy contributed 2,000 words of background information about the "Mahatmas," the Arbor Valley, and Ancient Wisdom.

> The "Mahatmas" or "Masters" are mentioned in the story more than once, although none of them appears. Personally, I have never met one to my certain knowledge, although this may be due to the fact that no one who really was a Mahatma or Master would dream of admitting it. I have met several men who claimed to be "Masters," but in each instance I have been quite sure the individual was an imposter (of which breed there are all too many); and I have met one man who, to judge by his conversation and his conduct, might have been one of them, but as he did not admit it, and I have no means of proving who or what he was, I can not lay claim to having seen one.

February 10	*Tros of Samothrace* (Britain; TR)	Novel
April 10	*The Enemy of Rome* (Britain; TR)	Novel
June 10	*Prisoners of War* (Britain; TR)	Novel
August 20	*Hostages to Luck* (Britain; TR)	Novel
October 10	*Admiral of Caesar's Fleet* (Britain; TR)	Novel
December 10	*The Dancing Girl of Gades* (Iberia; TR)	Novel

In the January 20 issue, Mundy authored a 550-word letter to the Camp-Fire in which he maintained that "Hunger is the source of crime." Less than a month later, the February 10 issue of *Adventure* carried the first story of the Tros series, Mundy's most important literary achievement. "Tros of Samothrace" was the first of six related tales to appear in *Adventure* during 1925. Combined with one additional episode published in that magazine in the following year, they became the massive 949-page volume, TROS OF SAMOTHRACE, published by Appleton-Century almost ten years later.

Early in 1924, Mundy's correspondence had revealed: "The next story is CLEOPATRA, and will include a character named Sait of Samothrace, who is picturesque, if nothing more. It will take at least six months to write." Sait grew into Tros, and the "Cleopatra" story was pushed to one side for the time being. Eventually, it was published in 1929 by the Bobbs-Merrill Company.

The appearance of Tros was a signal for the beginning of one of the most remarkable controversies in the history of American fiction magazines. *Adventure's* department, The Camp-Fire, was the vehicle that allowed authors, editors, and readers to voice their opinions, vent their likes and dislikes, or simply reminisce. In the February 10 issue, Arthur Sullivant Hoffman introduced this new series, while Mundy added 2,000 words by way of explanation and background concerning Caesar, ancient Britain, and the Samothracian Mysteries. He attacked popular historical beliefs about Caesar and the Roman Empire, and, quickly, the readership of *Adventure* was split into two camps: those for Talbot Mundy, and those against him.

> I have followed Caesar's Commentaries as closely as possible in writing this story, but as Caesar, by his own showing, was a liar, a brute, a treacherous humbug and conceited ass,

as well as the ablest military expert in the world at that time; and as there is plenty of information from ancient British, Welsh and Irish sources to refute much of what he writes, I have not been to much trouble to make him out a hero.

Rome rooted out and destroyed the (Samothracian) Mysteries and gave us in their place no spiritual guidance, but a stark materialism, the justification of war, and a world-hero — Caius Julius Caesar, the epileptic liar, who, by his own confession, slew at least three million men and gave their women to be slaves or worse, solely to further his own ambition. *Sic transit gloria Romae!*

To accompany "Prisoners of War," published in the June 10 issue, Mundy added another 1500 words of observation about ancient Britain and the Vikings. During the same month, in the June 30 issue, almost all of The Camp-Fire was enlisted for discussion of Mundy's Roman-Caesar theories. In that issue, and in the issues that followed, thousands of words were written in The Camp-Fire, and among those voicing opinions (none too gently) were authors Elmer Davis, Hugh Pendexter, Arthur D. Howden Smith, and Arthur Gilchrist Brodeur. Seven years earlier, Mundy had dedicated his book, HIRA SINGH, to Davis. In the July 10 issue, Mundy voiced another 3,000 words in reply to criticism from Mr. Howden Smith. On July 30, he added another 3,500 words of comment, and the August 20 issue, which featured "Hostages to Luck," provided 1500 words about ancient London, Druids, and Tros's methods of sea-warfare.

As the year wore on, more and more readers were attracted to the Mundy banner, and before the controversy had ended enough words had been published in The Camp-Fire to fill a large book. One can only conjecture at the total number of letters the magazine received.

In the October 30 issue, Arthur Sullivant Hoffman reported:

Lately the letters in the Caesar controversy have been almost wholly in support of Talbot Mundy. There is a whole lot more in the controversy than such matters as whether Caesar was or did this, that or the other. It brings out the questions of tolerance, how much thinking of our own we do, what are our measures of success and greatness, our ideals and the influence of commonly accepted ideals.

1926

February 10	*The Messenger of Destiny* (Rome; TR)	Serial, Part 1 of 3
February 20	*The Messenger of Destiny*	Serial, Part 2 of 3
February 28	*The Messenger of Destiny*	Serial, Part 3 of 3
June 8	*Ramsden* (Tibet; JG, JR, CG)	Serial, Part 1 of 5
June 23	*Ramsden*	Serial, Part 2 of 5
July 8	*Ramsden*	Serial, Part 3 of 5
July 23	*Ramsden*	Serial, Part 4 of 5
August 8	*Ramsden*	Serial, Part 5 of 5
October 23	*The Falling Star* (Rome; Commodus)	Novel

1926 was an important year for Talbot Mundy in *Adventure*. "The Messenger of Destiny," the final episode of Tros's conflict with Julius Caesar, appeared as a three-part serial in the February issues. In 1934 it was combined with six earlier exploits that had been published in 1925 to make up the book TROS OF SAMOTHRACE. Thereafter, Tros was missing from the pages of *Adventure* for a full ten years, and the magazine underwent a variety of changes in this period of time. They came almost immediately. Hoffman announced that three issues a month was simply too much reading for the magazine buyer, and with the April 8, 1926 issue, *Adventure* — it had been issued three times a month since October 1921 — reverted to a twice a month schedule. Also with the April 8 issue, announcement was made of the anthology ADVENTURE'S BEST STORIES to be published by the George H. Doran Company. It would include eighteen stories selected by the publisher and the *Adventure* editorial staff, and include "The Soul of a Regiment" by Talbot Mundy.

Capitalizing on the mystic appeal and the Oriental locale of "Om," the June 8 issue of *Adventure* commenced the five-part serial, "Ramsden." The characters were old Mundy favorites: Jimgrim, Ramsden, Chullunder Ghose, and Narayan Singh, with the latter meeting a violent, warrior's death. "Ramsden" was published in book form in the United States as THE DEVIL'S GUARD. A letter of 4,000 words by Talbot Mundy dealing with Eastern theory, *dugpas,* and philosophy accompanied "Ramsden" in the June 8 Camp-Fire.

In the September 23 issue, Hoffman reported — with obvious pleasure — that the ownership of the Ridgway Company, the publishers of *Adventure*, had been sold. Changes were promised, and they came quickly with the October 23 issue. To the dismay of many readers, the pictorial covers by such accomplished artists as Murphy, Ripley, and Heurlin were dropped in favor of bold type that proclaimed author and story content. However, the ground wood, "pulp" paper heretofore used in the magazine was eliminated in favor of an excellent white sheet that maintains its brightness and readability to this day. And more to the point, *Adventure*, for a time, continued on the high plane to which Arthur Sullivant Hoffman had brought it.

The October 23 issue featured Mundy's "The Falling Star," a fine tale of ancient Rome's warrior emperor, Commodus, which was later published in book form as CAESAR DIES.

1927

January 1	*The Red Flame of Erinpura* (India; CG)	Novel

The January 1 issue of Camp-Fire carried a 1,000-word biography of Talbot Mundy, an extract of which is printed below:

> As to Mundy, unless you know him extremely intimately you would never know that he had been farther away than around the corner. He talks well on every subject under the sun except Mundy for whom he seems to have a secret dislike. He is one of eight men in the world who can talk an infant into an instant giggle; strange dogs follow him in the street; he plays wretched poker and has a deep spirituality. . . .

In the February 1 issue, Arthur Sullivant Hoffman wrote:

> Will older readers ever forget the argument royal that arose among Camp-Fire over Talbot Mundy's interpretation of the character of Julius Caesar in the *Tros* stories? Had to stop it finally because it wasn't leaving space for much else, but I think most of us learned more about Julius Caesar than we had ever known before. We're still getting occasional requests to have the contributions to that argument issued in book form. Well, maybe we can someday.

1927 was a strange year for *Adventure* — a year of transition and unrest, which saw the publication of only one Talbot Mundy story, "The Red Flame of Erinpura." After his long relationship with Arthur Sullivant Hoffman, Mundy had to feel a deep personal loss in the change of editorship.

With the March 1 issue, designs and decorations for cover and interior pieces were assigned to the famous artist, Rockwell Kent. In April, Arthur Sullivant Hoffman announced that he would relinguish his much-loved Camp-Fire to Joseph Cox. Two months later, June 15, 1927, Hoffman wrote his farewell to *Adventure:*

To have been with *Adventure* ever since it was born in 1910, nearly nineteen years ago, and at last to say good-by makes something of an occasion, at least as far as I'm concerned. While I go of my own will, it is not possible to sever without a very real regret my relations not only with the magazine itself but with all of you who gather at Camp-Fire. We have met and talked together through the years, been friends, and saying good-by is not easy for me. So little easy that I shall say it briefly and have done.

Joseph Cox succeeded Hoffman as editor with the July 1 issue, and two weeks later the magazine returned to the cheaper, ground wood paper. However, the hew and outcry for full cover, illustrated covers had been heard, and they were restored with the August 1 issue. Within four months of the editorial change that placed Cox in the role of editor, Cox was gone, and Anthony Rud assumed the editorship on October 15.

1928

November 1	*The Wheel of Destiny* (India; QU)	Novelette
November 15	*The Big League Miracle* (India; QU)	Novelette
December 1	*On the Road to Allah's Heaven* (India: QU)	Novelette

Adventure's days of unrest continued into 1928, and Talbot Mundy was notably absent from its pages between January 1927 and November 1928. Evidence that not all was well with *Adventure* was provided in the January 1 issue by editor Anthony Rud:

> Several peculiar tales concerning *Adventure's* reversion to old policies have floated in of late. Except that some of our tried and true friends in the far places of the world have been distressed or angered, there would be no reason to do more than smile at these queer distortions of the truth. But let me say once and for all that the magazine is *not* disowning its old comrades; rather is it attempting to weld them more and more closely in pleasant bonds which only death may break. . . .

In the April 1 issue, Rud announced the results of a reader vote for the year 1927. "The Red Flame of Erinpura" placed fourth in the novelette category ("Rusudan" by Harold Lamb was most popular), while Talbot Mundy was selected third in author popularity. In the August 1 issue Rud had another announcement:

> Talbot Mundy — do I see a couple dozen of you chaps straighten up for a moment and forget to drag on the old briars? — is with us again after far too long an absence. A series of stories of India by him will start soon; and then we shall have a splendid serial novel in Mundy's best vein.

The new series commenced in the November 1 issue, and Mundy drew the following notice in The Camp-Fire:

In this issue appear — for the first time in many months, two of *Adventure's* old-time favorites, Talbot Mundy and Frederick J. Jackson. Mr. Mundy will continue this series of Ben Quorn, and the turbulent State of Narada. And following the fifth and final tale will start perhaps the finest story of Talbot Mundy's lifetime. It is a yarn of North India and South China — in which appears Jimgrim, Ramsden and the rest of the characters associated with them in the past. . . .

Portions of the first two Ben Quorn stories, "The Wheel of Destiny" and "The Big League Miracle," were re-written as a part of the book, THE GUNGA SAHIB. However, there are major differences in plot, and the popular Chullunder Ghose was cast as a character in the book, replacing an "inferior" babu of the magazine stories. Additional Ben Quorn exploits were published in the competitive magazine, *Argosy,* during 1929 and 1930.

Cover of *Adventure* magazine, November 1, 1928. Reproduced by permission of Popular Publications, Inc.

January 1	*Golden River* (India; QU)	Novelette
February 1	*A Tucket of Drums* (India; QU)	Novelette
February 15	*In Old Narada Fort* (India; QU)	Novelette
October 1	*The Invisible Guns of Kabul* (India)	Serial, Part 1 of 5
October 15	*The Invisible Guns of Kabul*	Serial, Part 2 of 5
November 1	*The Invisible Guns of Kabul*	Serial, Part 3 of 5
November 15	*The Invisible Guns of Kabul*	Serial, Part 4 of 5
December 1	*The Invisible Guns of Kabul*	Serial, Part 5 of 5

Mundy's inactivity during 1927 and most of 1928 was reflected in the reader polls. "The Wheel of Destiny" was selected as third choice in the short story category, while Mundy dropped to eleventh place among favorite authors.

The long serial, "The Invisible Guns of Kabul," was published in book form in the United States as COCK O' THE NORTH. In England the volume was called GUP BAHADUR.

February 1	*Consistent Anyhow* (Reincarnation)	Short Story
November 15	*King of the World* (Tibet; JG, JR)	Serial, Part 1 of 7
December 1	*King of the World*	Serial, Part 2 of 7
December 15	*King of the World*	Serial, Part 3 of 7

"The Invisible Guns of Kabul" placed second among *Adventure's* 1929 serials, while Mundy moved up to fourth in popularity among contributors.

Anthony Rud resigned as editor with the March 1 issue; he was replaced by A. A. Proctor. In the March 15 issue, the new editor wasted little time in posing a question to Mundy about Goorkha-Highlander relations. In a reply of 300 words, Mundy pointed out that the two held "an almost holy reverence for one another."

By July 1, Proctor was able to report on an unnamed Mundy story. The new work was identified as "King of the World" in the October 1 issue. "Mr. Mundy thinks it's one of the best things he's done, and the *Adventure* staff is inclined to agree with him." The seven-part serial began in the November 15 issue with a magnificent full-color cover by Hubert Rogers. "King of the World" is a Jimgrim-Ramsden novel which has its opening in southern Europe, moves to Egypt, and finally to an astonishing, science fiction climax in Tibet. Mundy chose to introduce it with a letter to The Camp-Fire of close to 2,000 words in which he pointed out:

> In Dorje I have imagined a mystic without one decent human instinct, who has come into possession of the scientific secrets of Atlantis, which provide him with such weapons as the world has never seen since lost Atlantis went under the waves. The secret of his near-success is as simple as the cause of his ultimate failure.

Cover of *Adventure* magazine, October 1, 1929. Reproduced
by permission of Popular Publications, Inc.

January 1	*King of the World*	Serial, Part 4 of 7
January 15	*King of the World*	Serial, Part 5 of 7
February 1	*King of the World*	Serial, Part 6 of 7
February 15	*King of the World*	Serial, Part 7 of 7
May 1	*Black Flag* (Pirates)	Short Story
August 1	*The Man on the Mat* (India)	Short Story
October 1	*The Babu* (India; CG, OH)	Short Story
November 15	*The Eye-Teeth of O'Hara* (India; OH)	Short Story

The final installments of "King of the World" appeared in the January and February issues of *Adventure,* and one month later the novel was published in book form as JIMGRIM under the imprint of the Century Company. "King of the World" is unique for, outwardly, it brings about the death of the most prolific of all the Mundy heroes, Jimgrim. However, when the question was voiced to Dawn Mundy, "Why did Talbot end Grim's life at this point — had he tired of him the way that Doyle tired of Sherlock Holmes?" she responded promptly. "He didn't. We talked this over and Talbot felt that he could bring Jimgrim back at any time . . . from a deep cavern or hiding place." Unfortunately, that time did not come.

Four short stories completed the output for *Adventure* in 1931. Three of the tales were set in India; the fourth involved the "brethren of the coast." *Adventure,* in its long and illustrious history, was strong on pirate yarns.

1932

January 1	*Case 13* (India; CG, OH)	Short Story
March 1	*Chullunder Ghose the Guileless* (India; CG)	Novelette
March 15	*A Jungle Sage* (Africa)	Article
April 1	*Watu* (Africa)	Article
August 1	*White Tigers* (India)	Serial, Part 1 of 2
August 15	*White Tigers*	Serial, Part 2 of 2

With Proctor as editor, Talbot Mundy continued his contributions to *Adventure* on a regular basis. Three stories and two articles appeared during 1932. "A Jungle Sage" and "Watu" were described as "Random Reminiscences of Africa," and called upon Mundy's personal experiences on the dark continent.

With the September 1 issue, the magazine was cut to 96 pages and the price reduced from 25¢ to 10¢; a sign of the bad times enveloping the country.

1933

March 1	*C.I.D.* (India; CG)	Serial, Part 1 of 4
March 15	*C.I.D.*	Serial, Part 2 of 4
April 1	*C.I.D.*	Serial, Part 3 of 4
April 15	*C.I.D.*	Serial, Part 4 of 4
August	*Red Sea Cargo* (Red Sea)	Short Story

C.I.D. was published in book form by the Century Company in November of 1932 — prior to the magazine serialization. The initials refer to Criminal Investigation Department.

In June 1933, *Adventure* became a monthly, increasing its price to 15¢ and adding another 32 pages to its format.

1935

May 1	*Battle Stations* (Mediterranean; TR)	Novelette
June 15	*Cleopatra's Promise* (Egypt; TR)	Novelette
August 15	*The Purple Pirate* (Egypt; TR)	Novelette
October 1	*Fleets of Fire* (Egypt; TR)	Novelette
November	*The Soul of a Regiment* (Egypt; dervishes)	Short Story

Talbot Mundy was absent from the pages of *Adventure* during the year 1934, and during this period the magazine underwent two changes in editorship. In March 1934, William Corcoran began a brief, six-month stint as editor. He was replaced by Howard V. L. Bloomfield.

Early in 1935 Bloomfield wrote:

> Talbot Mundy came in from Florida to talk things over. He has laid out a new series of historical yarns — Antony and Cleopatra this time — and is now beginning to write them.

"Battle Stations," the first of the final four tales in the exploits of Tros of Samothrace, appeared in the May 1 issue. It was accompanied by close to 1,000 words of explanation and comment by Mundy in The Camp-Fire. The June 15 Camp-Fire carried another 1300 words of fact and conjecture about Cleopatra and Ptolemaic Egypt, in which Mundy drew a parallel between Cleopatra and England's Queen Elizabeth.

> I have imagined Tros as a sort of spiritual ancestor of Sir Francis Drake, who could not possibly have got away for his famous voyage around the world without the queen's knowledge, consent and assistance. Like Elizabeth, Cleopatra was determined to hold her throne against all comers, at everyone's expense.

To accompany "The Purple Pirate" in the August 15 issue, Mundy devoted 700 words of The Camp-Fire to a comparison of Greek and Roman sportsmanship. With the final Tros episode in the October 15 issue, Mundy turned his considerations to Greek fire and early sea warfare.

The four Tros novelettes appearing in 1935 were joined together in book form as PURPLE PIRATE, published in October 1935 by the Appleton-Century Company.

November 1935 marked the 25th anniversary of *Adventure*, and once again the magazine became a monthly. It was increased to 176 pages, and the anniversary issue included a number of popular tales from its illustrious past. Mundy's "The Soul of a Regiment" was reprinted again, and former editor Arthur Sullivant Hoffman returned to write a history of the magazine.

November 1937	*Companions in Arms* (World War I)	Short Story
November 1940	*The Soul of a Regiment* (Egypt; dervishes)	Short Story
March 1941	*The Night the Clocks Stopped* (India)	Novelette
October 1954	*The Soul of a Regiment* (Egypt; dervishes)	Short Story

There were few contributions to *Adventure* in the last five years of Talbot Mundy's life, involved as he was with the popular radio program, *Jack Armstrong, the All-American Boy.* The October 1940 issue carried the following:

> Bad news comes from Florida just as we go to press — Talbot Mundy is dead.
>
> At the next Camp-Fire we will publish an account of his life and his stories.
>
> The next issue being our thirtieth anniversary, we had been casting about for one great story from the file of years to print once more for the veteran followers. Inevitably one story has come to mind, and there is now no question of the choice.
>
> Epitaph for Talbot Mundy: the most moving short story *Adventure* ever published — the story he sent us back in 1912 and called "The Soul of a Regiment."

The thirtieth anniversary issue of *Adventure*, dated November 1940, true to the editor's promise, carried a 1200-word account of Mundy's life which is reproduced here in part.

> When we saw him last, his heart was set on one great plan. He was going to ship a trailer, and a car, to India, and roam the Great Highway, that Kipling's *Kim* travelled. Perhaps he would never come back — there was so much to see, and learn. He unrolled all the rich colors and sights and sounds of that highway — paraded India right in front of you. Mundy could cast a spell when he talked of things like this. He knew exactly how that trailer must be made and equipped, and had designed it on paper.

In the same issue, a letter from the author Wyatt Blassingame, a neighbor of Mundy's, reveals something of those last days spent in Florida. The March 1941 Camp-Fire contained a letter from William R. Cox, another Florida writer, who related:

> . . . Down here, where he was a sort of genial, tough-fibred,
> kindly old household god to those of us fortunate enough
> to know him, his going was a hard thing. . . .

Adventure dragged along . . . its glory days all but forgotten, as one after another of its authors slipped away. "The Soul of a Regiment" was published one last time in October 1954. It was a last gasp for *Adventure,* the magazine that had printed so much fine material since its inception in 1910 and its glory days in the 1920's.

THE GLORY OF TROS

by Fritz Leiber

Talbot Mundy's *Tros of Samothrace* is one of the half-dozen novels I have re-read most often in the course of my life, or rather during the thirty-eight years since I first devoured it. Such books inevitably become parts of our lives, closely interwoven with all our thoughts and actions, and their re-reading a kind of personal religious rite, no matter how comfortably casual they feel at bedtime.

I recall when I first bought *Tros* seeing a great pyramid of the thick book-bricks in their bright yellow jackets touched with scarlet occupying all of a Denver department store window. That was in the autumn of 1934 when I was touring with my father's Shakespearean company its last season out, playing parts like Edgar in *King Lear* and Fortinbras in *Hamlet* — and doubling Marullus and Octavius in *Julius Caesar.* There's a linkage in that last, for *Tros* is a very long novel of historical adventure cleverly woven around Caesar's two abortive invasions of Britain, which he describes in Books IV and V of his *Commentaries* (which I had read in my second year of high school Latin — another cross-connection).

It was an exciting yet lonely time for me. I was hand-writing a Mayan lost-world adventure novel I never finished (we never got to the lost world) on hotel stationery, beginning with New York's Algonquin and ending with the Hollywood Hotel — though mostly I stayed at cheaper places. Thirty years later I captured some of the melancholy mood of that season in my novelette "Four Ghosts in Hamlet," though there the narrator's infatuation with Monica Singleton had a happier conclusion than my own timid romancings.

In high school I had been drawn to the sciences but rather repelled by history, due to the boring, loadedly patriotic repetition of the American variety, beginning with the spice trade and Columbus and ending with the Civil War and Reconstruction (the first event of supreme disinterest to a boy who hated pepper and the last a tissue of whitewash and untruth). But now, with *Tros,* a golden door to exciting vistas opened for me, and when next year (1935)

I read Robert Graves' *I Claudius,* that passageway to the past became permanently available for my imagination's wanderings.

Shortly thereafter I read the two other Tros books, *Queen Cleopatra* (where Tros is a minor character) and *Purple Pirate,* and they became almost equal favorites of mine, especially the second, which as it were sets the stage for another of Shakespeare's dramas, *Antony and Cleopatra.*

There's more connection than that between Shakespeare and Mundy. In his novels the latter favored large, long scenes, often of conferences, discussions, and debates, with the settings, actors, and costumes described in loving detail, very much in the manner of grand-opera theater. (As one result, my first science-fiction novel, *Gather Darkness!,* is full of orations and spectacle — and, yes, I started a Fafhrd-Mouser story involving the emperor Claudius.)

But of course the main attraction of Mundy's Roman novels is the character of Tros himself, a Greek mystic and man of action, who comes from the Aegean isle with his father to warn the Britons to resist Caesar at all costs. The two of them, along with Mundy's Druids, represent the mystery religions and secret brotherhoods of the east and a universal wisdom, to which Caesar opposes his fascist and totalitarian vision of Rome ruling the world — "A sort of imitation of nature with the fundamental truth of brotherhood and freedom left out! Caesar served his own ends, but he served Rome first." (Caesar is the villain of the book, a cruel and lecherous opportunist, but courageous, witty and charismatic. In the Cleopatra book Tros serves him and the queen without too many moral misgivings.) Tros' father belongs to a branch of the mystic brotherhoods that believes in nonviolent resistance to evil, Tros to a rather more practical branch which approves violence in a good cause after every effort has been made to avoid it and to mislead the enemy with honest but deceptive words.

Tros is an Odyssean character, by temperament an explorer seeking to widen horizons, whose ambition is to sail around the world, but also a freedom fighter who never breaks his word (though he is a serpent for guile). He says of himself, "Whence I came, I know. Whither I go, I know not. I came forth from the womb of Experience. What I know, that I am. What I know not, is the limitless measure of what I may become. Life grows and I see it. And so I grow because I know it. I will strike such a blow on the anvil of life as shall use to the utmost all I am. Thus, though I know not whither I go nor what I shall be, I shall go to no home of idleness. I shall be no gray ghost lamenting what I might have done, but did not."

You can imagine what trumpet words these were to a lonely, shy, introverted, and uncourageous young man (myself) who once solemnly described himself as a "nonfunctional idealist."

Tros on the other hand is a dauntless fighter, a swordsman without peer, and a resourceful leader of men, a wise disciplinarian who knows how to inspire men and win their affection. With women he is wary, though when he does commit himself to love, he does so monogamously and without reservations. Above all, he is a man who cannot pass by injustice. Even his passionate desire to circumnavigate the globe must wait on Caesar's defeat in the matter of Britain (and thereafter on various other commitments circumstance forces him to make).

And he is a doer! In the course of the book he outwits clever Caesar a half-dozen times, almost single-handedly beats a band of Northmen who become his faithful followers, and builds a supership that combines the best features of a three-masted sailing ship seventeen centuries ahead of its time and a galley with three banks of oars (and catapults that throw fused and bursting shells of Greek fire) — a pretty difficult combination, but made real in the book by the manner of telling and a wealth of loving detail. (One comes to love his palendromically named ship, *Liafail*, as much as Hornblower's *Lydia*.)

In short, Tros is a superman, but one made considerably more plausible and attractive than most by his scholarly and mystical abilities, his scientific and exploratory aspirations, and his willingness to grapple with moral problems, fight injustic, and succor the weak. In fact, I do believe that it was this idealism of Tros that made him so popular in the Thirties, when Fascism was on the rise and greed, duplicity, and cowardice seemed to rule the dealings of nations — much in the same way as Tolkien's *Lord of the Rings* appealed to a youth weary of similar conditions in the Fifties and Sixties. I know he appealed that way to me.

BOOKS

Talbot Mundy's first book was RUNG HO!, published on March 21, 1914 by Charles Scribner's Sons of New York. It was the only title by Mundy to be published by this concern. In 1916, The Bobbs-Merrill Company of Indianapolis began a long and effective association with Mundy with the publication of KING—OF THE KHYBER RIFLES. Essentially — with a pair of specialty edition exceptions — Bobbs-Merrill remained Mundy's American book publisher until 1930. Included among the titles published in this period were the very popular THE IVORY TRAIL (1919), OM / THE SECRET OF AHBOR VALLEY (1924), and THE DEVIL'S GUARD (1926). Bobbs-Merrill's final Mundy volume was BLACK LIGHT, published in October 1930.

By 1931, Mundy had become affiliated with The Century Company of New York who, in that year, published JIMGRIM and THE HUNDRED DAYS AND THE WOMAN AYISHA. A year later, Century merged with The D. Appleton Company to form D. Appleton-Century. Between 1932 and 1940, this firm produced such important works as TROS OF SAMOTHRACE (1934), PURPLE PIRATE (1935), and OLD UGLY FACE (1940).

On the other side of the Atlantic, Mundy's RUNG HO! was published by Cassell & Company a scant month after its American appearance in 1914. Cassell went on to publish editions of WINDS OF THE WORLD in 1916 and HIRA SINGH'S TALE (American title: HIRA SINGH) in 1918. Another London house, Constable & Company, published KING, OF THE KHYBER RIFLES (note the use of the comma in the title, as opposed to the American edition's dash [—]) in 1917 and THE IVORY TRAIL in 1920. Later in 1920, Hutchinson & Company published THE EYE OF ZEITOON. It was the first volume in an association that lasted the rest of Mundy's life. For a period of more than twenty-five years, no other English publisher would do a Mundy original until Andrew Dakers published the non-fiction volume, I SAY SUNRISE, in 1947.

This bibliography is concerned with English language editions originating in the two countries that first published Talbot Mundy — the United States and England — along with Canadian editions, which are essentially an outgrowth of the American and British. It is assembled in a form which we hope is self-explanatory. Book titles are noted on the first line in bold capitals. Where appropriate, contents of anthologies and collections follow. Definitive editions are listed numerically, and the initial printing states of both American and British editions are identified: binding descriptions, publication dates, illustrations, identifying notations, catalogue inclusions, etc. Finally, magazine titles, other book appearances under different titles, and a word or two describing the story locale, the era, and/or the protagonists complete the entry.

While the publications of The Century Company and, subsequently, The D. Appleton-Century Company are generally identifiable by the use of the words "First Printing" on the copyright page, or by a number one enclosed in parenthesis such, (1), on the final text page, The Bobbs-Merrill Company failed to use such a positive form of identification until the later years.

Most difficult of all the Talbot Mundy books to identify are those issued by Hutchinson & Company, the London publishing house that produced the greatest number of Talbot Mundy first editions. Records of this concern for the Mundy period appear to be no longer in existence, and it was not Hutchinson's practice to identify a book as a "First Edition" or "First Printing" with a notation on the copyright page. On the other hand, Hutchinson sometimes noted on the title page such information as "7th Thousand" or "Eleventh Thousand," indicating that a title had seen one or more earlier printings. This, of course, is an aid in establishing what is *not* a first edition, though is of no help at all in identifying what *is*.

Many of the Hutchinson publications carried a catalogue of books which immediately followed the last page of text. Catalogues were often dated — "Autumn 1933" or "Spring 1937," for example — and sometimes ran to as many as forty or fifty numbered pages. Frequently, the first printing of a book carried a catalogue which included a written description of that same volume. However, this was not always the case. Hutchinson first editions in this bibliography have been identified largely by inspection of those copies in the possession of the British Museum whose records establish a clear date of receipt corresponding to the publication date. Color binding and catalogue inclusions have also been taken from that source.

Dust wrappers reproduced by permission of:

The Bobbs-Merrill Company
Cassell Ltd.
Constable & Co., Ltd.
Doubleday & Company, Inc., for *Caves of Terror*, Garden City Publishing
    Company
E. P. Dutton, Inc., for publications of The Century Company and D. Appleton-
    Century Company
Hutchinson Corp.
Charles Scribner's Sons

AFFAIR IN ARABY
1. New York: Royal Books, (1953), pages 159. Paperback. (Bound with *Gonzaga's Woman* by John Jakes.)
Also published as *The King in Check*.
See also, "The King in Check," magazine appearance.
(Near-East; Jimgrim)

ALL FOUR WINDS
Being Four Long Novels of India.
Contents: *King, of the Khyber Rifles, Jimgrim, Black Light, Om.*
1. London: Hutchinson & Co., (1933), pages 1232. Black binding, yellow lettering. Contains Autumn 1933 catalogue.
See also "King, of the Khyber Rifles," "King of the World," and "Om," magazine appearances.

AVENGING LIAFAIL
1. New York: Zebra Books, 1976, pages 348. Paperback.
See also chapters 8-11 of "Prisoners of War," "Hostages to Luck," and chapters 1-12 of "Admiral of Caesar's Fleet," magazine appearances.
(Britain; Tros)

BLACK LIGHT
1. Indianapolis: The Bobbs-Merrill Co., (October) 1930, pages 315. Black binding, red lettering. States "First Edition."
2. London: Hutchinson & Co., (October 1930), pages 320. Red binding, black lettering. Contains Autumn 1930 catalogue.
3. Toronto: McClelland & Stewart, 1930, pages 315.
4. New York: A. L. Burt Co., (1931), pages 315.
5. New York: Bantam Books, 1978, pages 211. Introduction by Barbara Cartland. Paperback.
(First announced as *The Man from Jupiter.)*
Also published in the omnibus volume, *All Four Winds.*
Black Light was not published in magazine form.
(India)

Royal Books edition

Hutchinson edition

Bobbs-Merrill
edition (left)

Hutchinson
edition (right)

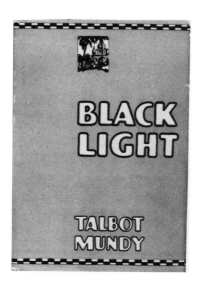

THE BUBBLE REPUTATION
By Talbot Mundy and Bradley King
1. London: Hutchinson & Co., (1923), pages 320. Dark red binding, black lettering. Contains Autumn 1923 catalogue.
2. London: Selwyn & Blount, (1933), pages 320.

Published in the United States as *Her Reputation*.

The Bubble Reputation was not published in magazine form.

(20th Century United States)

CAESAR DIES
1. London: Hutchinson & Co., (1934), pages 256. Red binding, black lettering. Contains Spring and Early Summer 1934 catalogue.
2. London: Hutchinson & Co., (c. 1937), pages 252. Paperback. #73 in Hutchinson's "Pocket Library."
3. New York: Centaur Books, Inc., 1973, pages 157. Paperback.

See also "The Falling Star," magazine appearance.

(Rome; Emperor Commodus)

CAVES OF TERROR
1. New York: Garden City Publishing Co., 1924, pages vi, 118. Frontis. and designs. Cover states: "NO. 62 / A Book for Boys." Paperback.
2. London: Hutchinson & Co., (1932), pages 255. Light gray binding, black lettering. Contains Spring 1932 catalogue.

See also "The Gray Mahatma," magazine appearance.

(India; King, Ramsden)

C.I.D.
1. London: Hutchinson & Co., (June 1932), pages 288. Yellow binding, black lettering. Contains Summer 1932 catalogue.
2. New York: The Century Co., (November) 1932, pages vi, 3-280. Yellow binding, black lettering. States "First Printing." [1]
3. New York: A. L. Burt Co., (1935), pages 286.
4. London: Hutchinson & Co., 1937, pages 256. Paperback. (Crime Book Society.)

See also "C.I.D.," magazine appearance.

(India; Chullunder Ghose)

Hutchinson edition

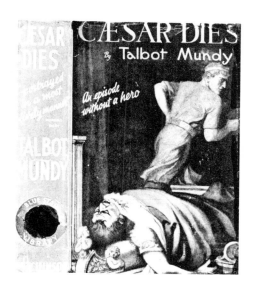

Garden City Publishing Co.
paperback edition

Century edition

COCK O' THE NORTH
1. Indianapolis: The Bobbs-Merrill Co., 1929, pages 340. Orange binding, black lettering. States "First Edition." *
2. Toronto: McClelland & Stewart, Ltd., 1929, pages 340.
3. New York: A. L. Burt Co., (1931), pages 340.

*Also exists in paperback state.
Published in England as *Gup Bahadur*.
See also "The Invisible Guns of Kabul," magazine appearance.
Seven pages of music, "In Some One's Heart," by Dawn Allen, follow the text.
(India; Northwest frontier)

THE DEVIL'S GUARD
1. Indianapolis: The Bobbs-Merrill Co., 1926, pages 335. Brown binding, green lettering.
2. New York: A. L. Burt Co., (1927), pages 335.
3. Philadelphia: The Oriental Club, 1945, pages 291. Foreword by Milton F. Wells.
4. New York: Avon Books, 1968, pages 255. Paperback.

Published in England as *Ramsden*.
See also "Ramsden," magazine appearance.
(India/Tibet; Jimgrim, Ramsden)

DIAMONDS SEE IN THE DARK
1. London: Hutchinson & Co., (1937), pages 287. Red binding, black lettering. Contains Autumn 1937 catalogue.

Published in the United States as *East and West*.
Diamonds See in the Dark was not published in magazine form.
(India)

EAST AND WEST
1. New York: D. Appleton-Century Co., 1937, pages v, 310. Yellow binding, black lettering. [1] [2]
2. Toronto: Ryerson Press, 1937, pages 310.

Published in England as *Diamonds See in the Dark*.
East and West was not published in magazine form.
(India)

Bobbs-Merrill
editions

Hutchinson edition

Appleton-Century edition

THE EYE OF ZEITOON
1. Indianapolis: The Bobbs-Merrill Co., (March) 1920, pages vii, 354. Frontis. and 3 illustrations by Dwight Franklin. Brown/tan binding, brown lettering.
2. London: Hutchinson & Co., (October 1920), pages 303. Red binding, black lettering. Contains Autumn 1920 catalogue.
3. New York: A. L. Burt Co., (1923), pages vii, 354. Frontis. by Dwight Franklin.
4. New York: McKinlay, Stone & Mackenzie, (1923), pages vi, 354. Frontis. by Dwight Franklin. [3]
5. Hutchinson & Co., (1929), pages 254. (The Leisure Library Co., Ltd.)

See also "The Eye of Zeitun," magazine appearance.
(Armenia/Turkey; Oakes, Yerkes, Montdidier)

FULL MOON
1. New York: D. Appleton-Century Co., 1935, pages vii, 312. Yellow binding, black lettering. [1] [2]
2. New York: Royal Books, (1953), pages 225. Paperback (Bound with *High Priest of California* by Charles Willeford.)

Published in England as *There Was a Door.*
See also "Full Moon," magazine appearance.
(India)

THE GUNGA SAHIB
1. London: Hutchinson & Co., (1933), pages 287. Red binding, black lettering. Contains Spring 1933 catalogue.
2. New York: D. Appleton-Century Co., 1934, pages vii, 303. Yellow binding, black lettering. States "First Printing." [1] [2]
3. New York: A. L. Burt Co., (1936), pages vii, 303.

Portions of *The Gunga Sahib* were published in magazine form as "The Wheel of Destiny," and "The Big League Miracle."
(India)

Bobbs-Merrill
edition (left)

Hutchinson
edition (right)

Reprint edition

Appleton-
Century
editions

GUNS OF THE GODS
1. Indianapolis: The Bobbs-Merrill Co., (June) 1921, pages vii 359. Frontis. and 5 illustrations by Joseph Clement Coll. Brown/tan binding, black lettering.
2. London: Hutchinson & Co. (November 1921), pages 288. Red binding, black lettering. Contains Autumn 1921 catalogue.
3. New York: A. L. Burt Co., (1923), pages vii, 359. Frontis. by Joseph Clement Coll.
4. New York: McKinlay, Stone & Mackenzie, (1923), pages vi, 359. Frontis. by Joseph Clement Coll. [3]
5. London: Hutchinson & Co., 1938, pages 252. Paperback (Hutchinson's Pocket Library.)

Also published in the omnibus volume, *Romances of India.*
See also "Guns of the Gods," magazine appearance.
(India; Yasmini)

GUP BAHADUR
1. London: Hutchinson & Co., (1929), pages 292. Blue binding, black lettering. No catalogue.

Published in the United States as *Cock o' the North.*
See also "The Invisible Guns of Kabul," magazine appearance.
(India, Northwest frontier)

HELENE
1. New York: Avon Books, 1967, pages 157. Paperback.
2. London: Tandem Books, 1971, pages 157. Paperback.

See also "The Messenger of Destiny," magazine appearance.
(Rome; Tros)

HELMA
1. New York: Avon Books, 1967, pages 240. Paperback.
2. London: Tandem Books, 1971, pages 140. Paperback.

See also "Prisoners of War" and "Hostages to Luck," magazine appearances.
(Britain; Tros)

Bobbs-Merrill edition

Hutchinson edition

HER REPUTATION
By Talbot Mundy and Bradley King
1. Indianapolis: The Bobbs-Merrill Co., (Photoplay Edition), 1923 page: ix, 333. Red binding, gold lettering.
2. New York: A. L. Burt Co., (Photoplay Edition), (1923), pages ix, 333.

Published in England as *The Bubble Reputation.*
The Photoplay Editions contain a frontis. and 3 interiors from the Thomas H Ince movie production.
Her Reputation was not published in magazine form.
(20th Century United States)

HIRA SINGH
1. Indianapolis: The Bobbs-Merrill Co., (September) 1918, pages vi, 308 Frontis. and 5 illustrations by Joseph Clement Coll. Olive green binding black lettering.
2. New York: A. L. Burt Co., (1923), pages vi, 308.
3. New York: McKinlay, Stone & Mackenzie, (1923), pages v, 308. Frontis by Joseph Clement Coll. [3]

Published in England as *Hira Singh's Tale.*
See also "Hira Singh's Tale," magazine appearance.
(World War I; Sikhs)

HIRA SINGH'S TALE
1. London: Cassell & Co., (June) 1918, pages 298. Brown binding, gold let tering. States "First Published 1918."
2. London: Hutchinson & Co., (1925), pages 288.

Published in the United States as *Hira Singh.*
See also "Hira Singh's Tale," magazine appearance.
(World War I; Sikhs)

THE HUNDRED DAYS
1. London: Hutchinson & Co., (1930), pages 255. Blue binding, black let tering. No catalogue.

Published in the United States as part of the volume *The Hundred Days and The Woman Ayisha.*
See also "Mohammad's Tooth," magazine appearance.
(Near-East; Jimgrim)

Bobbs-Merrill edition

Bobbs-Merrill edition

Hutchinson edition

THE HUNDRED DAYS AND THE WOMAN AYISHA*

1. New York: The Century Co., (1931), pages vii, 3-347. Yellow binding, black lettering. [2]

*Dust wrapper title: *"The Hundred Days."*
Published in England in two volumes: *The Hundred Days* and *The Woman Ayisha.*
See also "Mohammad's Tooth" and "The Woman Ayisha," magazine appearances.
(Near-East; Jimgrim)

I SAY SUNRISE

1. London: Andrew Dakers Ltd., 1947, pages xvii, 182. Blue binding, gold lettering. States "First Published 1947."
2. Philadelphia: Milton F. Wells, 1949, pages 187. Blue binding, gold lettering. States "First American Edition."
3. Toronto: S. J. R. Saunders, 1949, pages 187.
4. Los Angeles: DeVorss & Co., 1964, pages xvii, 182. Paperback.

I Say Sunrise was not published in magazine form.
(Non-fiction)

THE IVORY TRAIL

1. Indianapolis: The Bobbs-Merrill Co., 1919, pages v, 411. Frontis. and 5 illustrations by Joseph Clement Coll. Light brown binding, light brown lettering on dark brown panel; dark brown lettering on spine.
2. London: Constable & Co., 1920, pages 411. Frontis and 5 illustrations by Joseph Clement Coll. Green binding, dark green lettering.
3. New York: A. L. Burt Co., (1923), pages v, 411.
4. New York: McKinlay, Stone & Mackenzie, (1923), pages iv, 411. Frontis. by Joseph Clement Coll. [3]
5. London: Hutchinson & Co., (1925), pages 372.

Also published as *Trek East.*
See also "On the Trail of Tippoo Tib," magazine appearance.
(Africa; Oakes, Yerkes, Montdidier)

Century edition

Dakers edition
(left)

Wells edition
(right)

Bobbs-Merrill edition

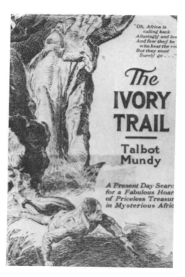

JIMGRIM
1. New York: The Century Co., (March) 1931, pages xiii, 3-385. Yellow bind ing, black lettering. States: "First Printing." [2]
2. London: Hutchinson & Co., (April 1931), pages 312. Red binding, black lettering. Contains Spring 1931 catalogue.
3. New York: A. L. Burt Co., (1933), pages xiv, 3-385.
4. New York: Avon Books, 1968, pages 288. Paperback.

Also published as *Jimgrim Sahib*.
Also published in the omnibus volume, *All Four Winds*.
See also "King of the World," magazine appearance.
(Europe, Africa, Asia; Jimgrim, Ramsden)

JIMGRIM AND ALLAH'S PEACE
1. London: Hutchinson & Co., (1933), pages 288. Red binding, black letter ing. Contains Supplementary Autumn 1933 catalogue.
2. New York: D. Appleton-Century Co., 1936, pages vi, 279. Yellow binding, black lettering. [1] [2]

See also "The Adventure at El-Kerak," and "Under the Dome of the Rock," magazine appearances.
(Near-East; Jimgrim)

JIMGRIM SAHIB
1. New York: Royal Books, (1953), pages 319. Paperback.

Also published as *Jimgrim*.
Also published in the omnibus volume, *All Four Winds*.
See also "King of the World," magazine appearance.
(Europe, Africa, Asia; Jimgrim, Ramsden)

JUNGLE JEST
1. London: Hutchinson & Co., (1931), pages 384. Blue binding, black letter ing. Contains Early Summer 1931 catalogue.
2. New York: The Century Co., (1932), pages vi, 3-392. Yellow binding, black lettering. States "First Printing." [2]

See also "Benefit of Doubt," "Treason," and "Diana Against Ephesians," mag azine appearances.
(India; Ommony, King)

Century edition

Hutchinson
edition (left)

Appleton-
Century
edition (right)

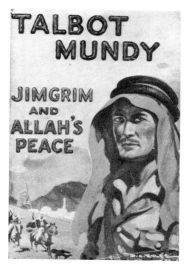 

Century edition

THE KING IN CHECK

1. London: Hutchinson & Co., (1933), pages 256. Red binding, black letter ing. Contains Spring 1933 catalogue.
2. New York: D. Appleton-Century Co., 1934, pages v, 244. Purple binding gold stamping. (Tired Business Man's Library of Adventure, Detective and Mystery Novels.) [1]
3. Toronto: Ryerson Press, 1934, pages 244.
4. New York: A. L. Burt Co., (1936), pages 244.

Also published as *Affair in Araby*.

See also "The King in Check," magazine appearance.

(Near-East; Jimgrim, Ross, Ramsden)

KING—OF THE KHYBER RIFLES

1. Indianapolis: The Bobbs-Merrill Co., 1916, pages v, 395. Olive binding gold lettering. Frontis. and 6 doublespread illustrations by Joseph Clemen Coll. Title page misspells Mundy's name "Talbott."
2. New York: A. L. Burt Co., (1923), pages iii, 395.
3. New York: McKinlay, Stone & Mackenzie, (1923), pages iv, 395. Frontis by Joseph Clement Coll. [3]
4. New York: Grosset & Dunlap, 1942, pages 395. (Madison Square Books.)
5. West Kingston, R.I.: Donald M. Grant, 1978, pages ix, 394. With 30 illus trations and numerous page designs by Joseph Clement Coll. Introduction by Donald M. Grant.

Published in England as *King, of the Khyber Rifles*. Also published in the United States as *King of the Khyber Rifles*.

Also published in the omnibus volume, *Romances of India*.

Also published in the omnibus volume, *All Four Winds*.

See also "King, of the Khyber Rifles," magazine appearance.

(India, Northwest frontier; King, Yasmini)

Hutchinson edition

Appleton-Century edition

Bobbs-Merrill edition

KING, OF THE KHYBER RIFLES
1. London: Constable & Co., 1917, pages iii, 344. Frontis. and 6 doublespread illustrations by Joseph Clement Coll. Blue binding, red lettering.
2. London: Hutchinson & Co., (1925), pages 304.
3. London: Tom Stacey, Ltd., 1973, pages 320.

Published in the United States as *King—of the Khyber Rifles* and *King of the Khyber Rifles*.

Also published in the omnibus volume, *Romances of India*.

Also published in the omnibus volume, *All Four Winds*.

See also "King, of the Khyber Rifles," magazine appearance.

(India, Northwest frontier; King, Yasmini)

KING OF THE KHYBER RIFLES
1. New York: Beacon Books, (1954), pages 288. Paperback. "Uncensored Edition."

Published in England as *King, of the Khyber Rifles*.

Also published in the United States as *King—of the Khyber Rifles*.

Also published in the omnibus volume, *Romances of India*.

Also published in the omnibus volume, *All Four Winds*.

See also "King, of the Khyber Rifles," magazine appearance.

(India, Northwest frontier; King, Yasmini)

LIAFAIL
1. New York: Avon Books, 1967, pages 255. Paperback.
2. London: Tandem Books, 1971, pages 255. Paperback.

See also "Admiral of Caesar's Fleet" and "The Dancing Girl of Gades," magazine appearances.

(Europe; Tros)

THE LION OF PETRA
1. London: Hutchinson & Co., (1932), pages 255. Red binding, black lettering. Contains Summer 1932 catalogue.
2. New York: D. Appleton-Century Co., 1933, pages v, 3-247. Yellow binding, black lettering. [2]

See also "The Lion of Petra," magazine appearance.

(Near-East; Jimgrim)

Beacon Books edition

Appleton-Century edition

THE LOST TROOPER

1. London: Hutchinson & Co., (1931), pages 255. Brownish-yellow binding, black lettering. Contains Autumn 1931 catalogue.

See also "The Lost Trooper," magazine appearance.

(Near-East; Jimgrim)

LUD OF LUNDEN

1. New York: Zebra Books, 1976, pages 377. Paperback.

See also "Tros of Samothrace," "The Enemy of Rome," and chapters 1-7 of "Prisoners of War," magazine appearances.

(Britain; Tros)

THE MARRIAGE OF MELDRUM STRANGE

1. London: Hutchinson & Co., (1930), pages 254. Red binding, black lettering. Contains Spring 1930 catalogue.

See also "The Marriage of Meldrum Strange," magazine appearance.

(India; Ommony, Strange, Ramsden, Chullunder Ghose)

THE MYSTERY OF KHUFU'S TOMB

1. London: Hutchinson & Co., (1933), pages 253. Red binding, black lettering. Contains Summer 1933 catalogue.
2. New York: D. Appleton-Century Co., 1935, pages vi, 279. Purple cloth, gold lettering. (Tired Business Man's Library of Adventure, Detective, and Mystery Novels.) [1]

See also "Khufu's Real Tomb," magazine appearance.

(Egypt; Jimgrim, Ramsden, Strange)

Hutchinson edition

Hutchinson edition

Appleton-Century edition

THE NINE UNKNOWN

1. Indianapolis: The Bobbs-Merrill Co., (March) 1924, pages vi, 353. Blue binding, blue lettering on yellow panel. Chapter heading designs.
2. London: Hutchinson & Co., (June 1924), pages 301. Red binding, black lettering. Contains Spring 1924 catalogue.
3. New York: McKinlay, Stone & Mackenzie, (c. 1924), pages iv, 353. Frontis. by Joseph Clement Coll. (Frontis. is the same illustration that faces page 108 of the Bobbs-Merrill edition of *Guns of the Gods.*) [3]
4. New York: A. L. Burt Co., (1925), pages vi, 353.
5. New York: Avon Books, 1968, pages 254. Paperback.

See also "The Nine Unknown," magazine appearance.

(India; Jimgrim, Ramsden, Ross, King, Chullunder Ghose)

OLD UGLY FACE

1. New York: D. Appleton-Century Co., (February) 1940, pages vi, 544. Green binding, gold lettering. [1]
2. London: Hutchinson & Co., (June 1940), pages 608. Pink binding, white lettering. Contains undated catalogue.
3. Toronto: Ryerson Press, 1940, pages vi, 544.
4. Philadelphia: Wells & Shakespeare, 1950, pages vi, 544.

See also "Old Ugly Face," magazine appearance.

(Tibet)

Bobbs-Merrill edition

Appleton-Century edition

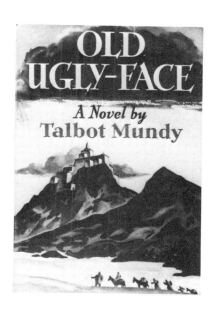

OM / THE SECRET OF AHBOR VALLEY

1. Indianapolis: The Bobbs-Merrill Co., 1924, pages viii, 3-392. Green binding, black lettering.
2. London: Hutchinson & Co., 1925, pages 352. Red binding, black lettering. Contains 1925 catalogue.
3. New York: McKinlay, Stone & Mackenzie, (c. 1924), pages vi, 392. Frontis.: photograph of Talbot Mundy. [3]
4. New York: A. L. Burt Co., (1926), pages vi, 392.
5. Point Loma, Ca.: Theosophical Press, 1931, pages vi, 392.
6. New York: Crown Publishers, (1962), pages vi, 392. Paperback. (Xanadu Library.)
7. New York: Avon Books, 1967, pages 336. Paperback.
8. London: Cedric Chivers, Ltd., 1968, pages 348.
9. San Diego: Point Loma Publications, 1980, pages viii, 3-392. Paperback. Introduction by Peter Berresford Ellis.

Also published in the omnibus volume, *All Four Winds.*
See also "Om," magazine appearance.
(India; Northwest frontier; Ommony)

THE PRAETOR'S DUNGEON

1. New York: Zebra Books, 1976, pages 396. Paperback.

See also chapters 13-15 of "Admiral of Caesar's Fleet," "The Dancing Girl of Gades," and "The Messenger of Destiny," magazine appearances.
(Europe; Tros)

PURPLE PIRATE

1. New York: D. Appleton-Century Co., (October 1935, pages viii, 367. Yellow binding, black lettering. [1] [2]
2. London: Hutchinson & Co., (November 1935), pages 496. Purple binding, gold lettering. Contains Autumn 1935 catalogue.
3. Toronto: Ryerson Press, (1935), pages 367.
4. Hicksville, N.Y.: Gnome Press, 1959, pages viii, 367.
5. Toronto: Burns & MacEachern, 1967, pages 367.
6. New York: Avon Books, 1970, pages 384. Paperback.

Also published as *The Purple Pirate.*
See also "Battle Stations," "Cleopatra's Promise," "The Purple Pirate," and "Fleets of Fire," magazine appearances.
(Egypt; Tros, Cleopatra)

Bobbs-Merrill
editions

 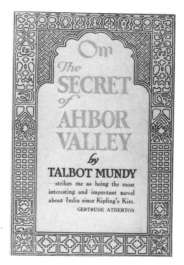

Hutchinson edition

Appleton-Century edition

THE PURPLE PIRATE
1. New York: Zebra Books, 1977, pages 377. Paperback.
Also published as *Purple Pirate*.
See also "Battle Stations," "Cleopatra's Promise," "The Purple Pirate," and "Fleets of Fire," magazine appearances.
(Egypt; Tros, Cleopatra)

QUEEN CLEOPATRA
1. Indianapolis: The Bobbs-Merrill Co., (February) 1929, pages xi, 426. Black binding, green lettering. States "First Edition."
*2. Indianapolis: The Bobbs-Merrill Co., (February) 1929, pages xi, 426. Brown boards, dark blue spine; brown lettering on white label. Frontis.: photograph of author.
3. London: Hutchinson & Co. (March 1929), pages 320. Red binding, black lettering. Contains Spring 1929 catalogue.
4. New York: Avon Books, 1959, pages 335. Paperback.
5. New York: Ace Books, 1962, pages 319. Paperback.
6. New York: Zebra Books, 1978, pages vi, 426. Paperback.
*States: "This special edition of *Queen Cleopatra* is limited to two hundred and sixty-five copies of which two hundred and fifty are for sale. Each is signed by the author. This is No. ____."
Queen Cleopatra was not published in magazine form.
(Egypt; Cleopatra, Tros)

THE QUEEN'S WARRANT
1. New York: Royal Books, (1953), pages 137. (Bound with *Paths of Glory* by Humphrey Cobb.) Paperback.
Cover title: *The Queen's Warrant / W.H.*
Published in England as *W.H.*
See also "Ho for London Town," magazine appearance.
(England; 1585)

RAMSDEN
1. London: Hutchinson & Co., (1926), pages 287. Slate green binding, black lettering. Contains Spring 1926 catalogue.
Published in the United States as *The Devil's Guard*.
See also "Ramsden," magazine appearance.
(India/Tibet; Jimgrim, Ramsden)

Bobbs-Merrill
edition (left)

Hutchinson
edition (right)

Royal Books edition

Hutchinson edition

THE RED FLAME OF ERINPURA

1. London: Hutchinson & Co., (1934), pages 255. Red binding, black lettering. Contains Spring 1934 catalogue.

See also "The Red Flame of Erinpura," magazine appearance.

(India; Chullunder Ghose)

ROMANCES OF INDIA

Contents: *King—of the Khyber Rifles, Guns of the Gods, Told in the East.*

1. New York: A. L. Burt Co., (1936), pages 1033. Orange binding, black lettering.
2. Toronto: McClelland & Stewart, (1936), pages 1033.

RUNG HO!

1. New York: Charles Scribner's Sons, (March) 1914, pages iii, 3-371. Green binding, black lettering; gold lettering on spine. States "Published March 1914."
2. London: Cassell & Co., (April) 1914, pages ii, 350. Blue binding, gold lettering.
3. New York: A. L. Burt Co., (1923), pages iv, 3-371.
4. New York: McKinlay, Stone & Mackenzie, (1923), pages iii, 3-371. Frontis. by Joseph Clement Coll. (Frontis. is the same illustration that faces page 90 of the Bobbs-Merrill edition of *Hira Singh.*) [3]
5. London: Hutchinson & Co., (1925), pages 319.

See also "Rung Ho!," magazine appearance.

(India)

THE SEVENTEEN THIEVES OF EL-KALIL

1. London: Hutchinson & Co., (1935), pages 254. Red binding, black lettering. No catalogue.

See also "The Seventeen Thieves of El-Kalil," magazine appearance.

(Near-East; Jimgrim)

Hutchinson edition

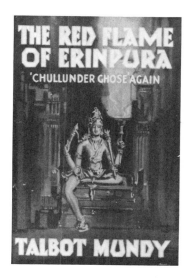

Scribner's
edition

Hutchinson edition

THE SOUL OF A REGIMENT

1. San Francisco: Alex Dulfer Printing Co., 1925, pages 25. Blue green boards with blue lettering; white spine, no lettering on spine. Introduction by Franklin F. Kenney.

The Dulfer edition is a separate book appearance of this short story.
Also published in the short story collection, *The Valiant View.*
See also "The Soul of a Regiment," magazine appearance.
(Egypt; dervishes)

THERE WAS A DOOR

1. London: Hutchinson & Co., (1933), pages 287. Red binding, black lettering. Contains Autumn 1933 catalogue.
2. Toronto, Ryerson Press, 1936, pages 287.

Published in the United States as *Full Moon.*
See also "Full Moon," magazine appearance.
(India)

THE THUNDER DRAGON GATE

1. London: Hutchinson & Co., (March 1937), pages 287. Red binding, black lettering. Contains Spring 1937 catalogue.
2. New York: D. Appleton-Century Co., 1937, pages vii, 335. Yellow binding, black lettering. [1] [2]
3. Toronto: Ryerson Press, 1937, pages 287.

See also "The Thunder Dragon Gate," magazine appearance.
(India, Northwest frontier)

TOLD IN THE EAST

Contents: "Hookum Hai," "For the Salt Which He Had Eaten," "MacHassan Ah."

1. Indianapolis: The Bobbs-Merrill Co., pages v, 281. Light brown binding, light brown lettering on black panel; black lettering on spine.
2. New York: McKinlay, Stone & Mackenzie, (1923), pages iv, 281. Frontis. by Joseph Clement Coll. (Frontis. is the same illustration that faces page 284 of the Bobbs-Merrill edition of *The Ivory Trail.)* [3]

Also published in the omnibus volume, *Romances of India.*
See also "Hookum Hai," "For the Salt Which He Had Eaten," and "MacHassan Ah," magazine appearances.
(India)

Hutchinson edition

Hutchinson
edition (left)

Appleton-
Century
edition (right)

Bobbs-Merrill edition

TREK EAST
1. New York: Royal Books, (1953), pages 319. Paperback.
Also published as *The Ivory Trail.*
See also "On the Trail of Tippoo Tib," magazine appearance.
(Africa; Oakes, Yerkes, Montdidier)

TROS
1. New York: Avon Books, 1967, pages 239. Paperback.
2. London: Tandem Books, 1971, pages 239. Paperback.
See also "Tros of Samothrace," and "The Enemy of Rome," magazine appearances.
(Britain; Tros)

TROS OF SAMOTHRACE
1. New York: D. Appleton-Century Co., (September) 1934, pages viii, 949. Yellow binding, black lettering. [1] [2]
2. London: Hutchinson & Co., (October 1934), pages 960. Black binding, blue-green lettering. Contains August 1934 catalogue.
3. Hicksville, N.Y.: Gnome Press, 1958, pages viii, 949.
4. London: Cedric Chivers Ltd., 1968, pages 960.
See also "Tros of Samothrace," "The Enemy of Rome," "Prisoners of War," "Hostages to Luck," "Admiral of Caesar's Fleet," "The Dancing Girl of Gades," and "The Messenger of Destiny," magazine appearances.
(Europe; Tros)

Royal Books edition

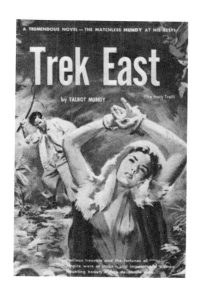

Appleton-Century edition

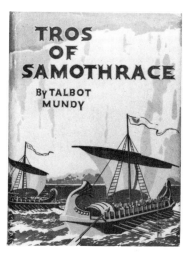

Hutchinson
edition

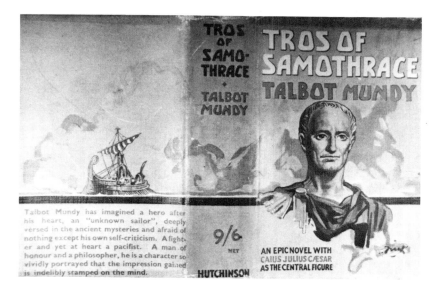

THE VALIANT VIEW
Contents: "The Soul of a Regiment," "The Damned Old Nigger," "The Chaplain of Mullingars," "The Pillar of Light," "An Arabian Night," "MacHassan Ah," "The Man From Poonch," "The Eye-Teeth of O'Hara," "Innocent Noncombatant," "Honorable Pig."
  1. London: Hutchinson & Co., (1939), pages 256. Red binding, black lettering. Contains undated catalogue.
(Short story collection)

W.H. / A Portion of the Record of Sir William Halifax
  1. London: Hutchinson & Co., (1931), pages 256. Orange binding, brown lettering. No catalogue.
Published in the United States as *The Queen's Warrant.*
See also "Ho for London Town," magazine appearance.
(England; 1585)

WHEN TRAILS WERE NEW
  1. London: Hutchinson & Co., (1932), pages 288. Light brown binding, brown lettering. Contains Early Spring 1932 catalogue.
See also "When Trails Were New," magazine appearance.
(American historical; Black Hawk War)

Hutchinson edition

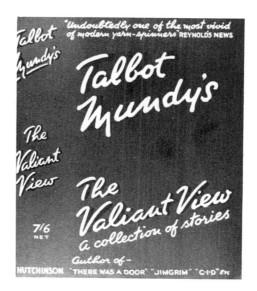

Hutchinson edition

Hutchinson edition

THE WINDS OF THE WORLD
1. London: Cassell & Co., 1916, pages 310. Red binding, black lettering.
2. Indianapolis: The Bobbs-Merrill Co., 1917, pages v, 331. Frontis. and 4 illustrations by Joseph Clement Coll. Orange/brown binding, black lettering.
3. Toronto: George J. McLeod, 1917, pages v, 331. Illustrated by Joseph Clement Coll.
4. New York: McKinlay, Stone & Mackenzie, (1923), pages v, 331. Frontis. by Joseph Clement Coll. [3]
5. New York: A. L. Burt Co., (1923), pages iv, 331. Frontis. by Joseph Clement Coll.
6. London: Hutchinson & Co., (1925), pages 285.

See also "The Winds of the World," magazine appearance.
(India; Yasmini)

THE WOMAN AYISHA
1. London: Hutchinson & Co., (1930), pages 256. Red cloth, black lettering. No catalogue.

Published in the United States as part of the volume *The Hundred Days and The Woman Ayisha.*
See also "The Woman Ayisha," magazine appearance.
(Near-East; Jimgrim)

---

[1] First printing indicated by the number one enclosed in parenthesis such, (1), on the final page of text.

[2] A mysterious Oriental figure ponders over a world globe. Front cover of binding, lower right.

[3] Nine Talbot Mundy titles were published by McKinlay, Stone and Mackenzie in matched bindings. McKinlay, Stone and Mackenzie was an affiliate of Review of Reviews (Hearst), and sales of these editions were primarily mail order.

Bobbs-Merrill edition

Burt edition

Hutchinson edition

ANTHOLOGIES

ADVENTURE'S BEST STORIES
New York: Doran, 1926. Contains "The Soul of a Regiment."

MY BEST ADVENTURE STORY
London: Faber & Faber, 1934. Contains "The Soul of a Regiment."

MY BEST SPY STORY
London: Faber & Faber, 1938. Contains "The Piping Dreams of Peace."

MY MOST EXCITING STORY
London: Faber & Faber, 1936. Contains "The Bell on Hell Shoal."

MY BEST THRILLER
London: Faber & Faber, 1935. Contains "The Gods Seem Content."

OTHER BOOK APPEARANCES

A CURIOUS LIFE by George Wehner.
New York: Liveright, 1929.
Introduction by Talbot Mundy.

FICTION WRITERS ON FICTION WRITING, edited by Arthur Sullivant Hoffman.
Indianapolis: The Bobbs-Merrill Co., 1929.
Contains "Talbot Mundy on Fiction Writing."

WINE OF LIFE by Katherine A. Tingley.
Point Loma, CA., Theosophical Publishing Company, 1925.
Preface by Talbot Mundy.

MAGAZINE APPEARANCES

The following is an attempt to list the magazine appearances — both fiction and non-fiction — of Talbot Mundy as printed in the United States, England, and Canada. Entries are listed alphabetically for easy referral, with the title set in bold capitals, and the periodicals in italics. Articles, serials, and poems are noted in parentheses, and book appearances are listed immediately below the entry. In the case of serialization, the date of the initial appearance is noted. British and Canadian magazines are identified by (Br.) and (Can.), respectively.

In some instances the magazine story is not the total content of the book noted. Such an example is "Admiral of Caesar's Fleet" which is only one portion of the book, *Tros of Samothrace*. Another example, "An Arabian Night," is a complete story within itself, and only one of the tales included in the volume, *Told in the East*. No attempt is made in this section to identify the total content of a book. However, the interested reader may find these facts by referral to the section entitled "Book Appearances."

Walter Galt is the one known pseudonym used by Talbot Mundy in his writing career, and magazine appearances employing this byline are noted. (Walter Galt Gribbon was Mundy's father.) Interestingly, some of the tales authored by "Walter Galt," which appeared in the United States in the early days of *Adventure* magazine, were published in Mundy's native Britain with the byline "Talbot Mundy."

Every attempt to list all of Mundy's magazine output has been made in this volume. However, since so much of Mundy's writing appeared for the first time in *Adventure* magazine, a chronological listing of material *by* and *about* Mundy is included in the section of this book entitled "Talbot Mundy in *Adventure*." This includes anecdotes, letters, autobiographies, and explanations not included in this section.

Another independent section is devoted to "Talbot Mundy in *The Theosophical Path*," a magazine published by Katherine Tingley's theosophist movement originating in Point Loma, California. During one period of the 1920's, Mundy was a regular contributor to this magazine.

The Crescent (see "The Real Red Root" and "Peter from Paradise Bend") was "A Monthly Magazine published at St. Paul, Minn., in the interest of the Ancient Arabic Order, Nobles Mystic Shrine by The Crescent Publishing Company."

ACROSS THE COLOR LINE (by Walter Galt)
Adventure: October 1912

ADMIRAL OF CAESAR'S FLEET
Adventure: October 10, 1925
Book: TROS OF SAMOTHRACE
Book: AVENGING LIAFAIL, Chapters 1-12
Book: THE PRAETOR'S DUNGEON, Chapters 13-15

THE ADVENTURE AT EL-KERAK
Adventure: November 10, 1921
Book: JIMGRIM AND ALLAH'S PEACE

THE AFFAIR AT KALIGAON (3-part serial)
Argosy: May 24, 1930

AMERICA HORNS IN
Adventure: First January 1919

ANOTHER'S DUTY IS FULL OF DANGER (article)
The Theosophical Path: July 1924

AN ANSWER TO CORRESPONDENTS (article)
The Theosophical Path: January 1925

APOLOGY (article)
The Theosophical Path: January 1926

AN ARABIAN NIGHT
  Adventure: November 1913
  Book: TOLD IN THE EAST

ARMENIA (verse)
  New York Times Current History: August 1920

THE ART OF DYING DAILY (article)
  (Also published as "Spiritual Man Is Eternal: There Are No Dead")
  The Eclectic Theosophist: Sept.-Oct. 1980

ASOKA'S ALIBI (3-part serial)
  Argosy All-Story: March 9, 1929

AS TO CAPITAL PUNISHMENT (article)
  The Theosophical Path: December 1925

AS TO SUCCESS & FAILURE (article)
  The Theosophical Path: April 1925

AS TO WRITING AND READING (article)
  The Theosophical Path: February 1925

AT MANEUVERS
  Adventure: June 1913

THE AVENGER
  This Week: May 16, 1937

THE BABU
  Adventure: October 1, 1931

BARABBAS ISLAND
  Adventure: Mid-October 1919

BATTLE STATIONS
Adventure: May 1, 1935
Book: PURPLE PIRATE

A BEGINNER'S CONCEPT OF THEOSOPHY (article)
The Theosophical Path: May 1925

THE BELL ON HELL SHOAL
The Passing Show (Br.): July 15, 1933
Book: MY MOST EXCITING STORY

BENEFIT OF DOUBT
Adventure: December 10, 1922
Book: JUNGLE JEST

BENGAL REBELLION
Blue Book: January 1935

THE BIG LEAGUE MIRACLE
Adventure: November 15, 1928

BILLY BLAIN EATS BISCUITS (by Walter Galt)
Adventure: January 1916

BILLY BLAIN'S ONIONS AND GARLIC (by Walter Galt)
Adventure: February 1916

BLACK FLAG
Adventure: May 1, 1931

BLACKMAIL (article)
The Theosophical Path: June 1924

"BLIGHTY" (article)
Adventure: Mid-August 1918

THE BLOODING OF THE NINTH QUEEN'S OWN
Adventure: December 1911
The Grand (Br.): August 1912

BROTHERHOOD OR LEAGUE? (article)
The Theosophical Path: October 1923

BURBETON AND ALI BEG
Everybody's: January 1914
New Magazine (Br.): August 1914
Argosy (Br.): August 1927

BY ALLAH WHO MADE TIGERS (3-part serial)
Argosy All-Story: April 27, 1929

CAMERA!
Argosy: January 6, 1934

CASE 13
Adventure: January 1, 1932
Britannia & Eve (Br.): August 1932

CHANT (verse)
The Theosophical Path: August 1924

THE CHAPLAIN OF THE MULLINGARS
Adventure: March 1912
Pall Mall (Br.): June 1912
Book: THE VALIANT VIEW

CHRISTENING CANNON ROCK
Cavalier: February 10, 1912

CHULLUNDER GHOSE THE GUILELESS
Adventure: March 1, 1932

C.I.D. (4-part serial)
Adventure: March 1, 1933
Book: C.I.D.

CIVILIZATION, ART AND SAN DIEGO (article)
San Diego Magazine: September 1927

CLEOPATRA'S PROMISE
Adventure: June 15, 1935
Book: PURPLE PIRATE

CLIMATE AND CONDITIONS: A RED SEA RHAPSODY
Pall Mall (Br.): April 1913

THE CLOSED TRAIL OF WILLIAM WALKER (article)
Adventure: August 1913

COMPANION IN ARMS
Adventure: November 1937

CONSISTENT ANYHOW
Adventure: February 1, 1930

CORNELIA'S ENGLISHMAN
The All-Story: September 1911

THE COWARDS
Adventure: July 1912

THE DAMNED OLD NIGGER
Adventure: May 1917
Book: THE VALIANT VIEW

THE DANCING GIRL OF GADES
Adventure: December 10, 1925
Book: TROS OF SAMOTHRACE
Book: THE PRAETOR'S DUNGEON

DIANA AGAINST EPHESIANS
Adventure: August 10, 1923
Book: JUNGLE JEST

DICK ANTHONY OF ARRAN: THE SWORD OF ISKANDER
Adventure: August 1914

DISOWNED!
Adventure: January 1915

DORG'S LUCK (by Walter Galt)
Adventure: August 1912

THE DOVE WITH A BROKEN WING
Adventure: June 1915
New Magazine (Br.): October 1915
The Storyteller (Br.): November 1937

A DROP OR TWO OF WHITE
Adventure: February 1916
Golden Book: September 1925

EASTERN PROVERB (verse)
The Theosophical Path: April 1924

ELEPHANT HUNTING FOR A LIVING (article) (by Walter Galt)
Adventure: July 1912

ELEPHANT HUNTING FOR A LIVING (article) (by Talbot Mundy)
Pall Mall (Br.): February 1913

ELEPHANT SAHIB (6-part serial)
Argosy: December 6, 1930

THE ELEPHANT WAITS
Short Stories: February 25, 1937
Short Stories (Br.): Mid-June 1937
Short Stories: February 1959

THE EMPTY SADDLE
(Also published as "For the Salt Which He Had Eaten")
The Storyteller (Br.): June 1913

THE END OF THE BAD SHIP BUNDESRATH
Adventure: Mid-April 1919

THE ENEMY OF ROME
Adventure: April 10, 1925
Book: TROS OF SAMOTHRACE
Book: LUD OF LUNDEN

EXCERPT FROM TROS OF SAMOTHRACE
Traces — A Driving Magazine: February 15, 1977 (Vol. 1, No. 1)

THE EYE TEETH OF O'HARA
Adventure: November 15, 1931
Book: THE VALIANT VIEW

THE EYE OF ZEITUN (2-part serial)
Romance: February 1920
Book: THE EYE OF ZEITOON

THE FALLING STAR
Adventure: October 23, 1926
Book: CAESAR DIES

FATA VIRUMQUE CANO (verse)
The Theosophical Path: June 1924

THE FIRE COP
The Scrap Book: October 1911

FLAME OF CRUELTY
Romance: August 1929

FLEETS OF FIRE
  Adventure: October 1, 1935
  Book: PURPLE PIRATE

FOR THE PEACE OF INDIA (3-part serial)
  Adventure: February 1914
  Book: RUNG HO!

FOR THE SALT WHICH HE HAD EATEN
  (Also published as "The Empty Saddle")
  Adventure: March 1913
  Book: TOLD IN THE EAST

FOR VALOUR
  Adventure: January 1912

FOUL OF THE CZAR
  Adventure: September 1914

FRANCIS BANNERMAN—A MAN OF MYSTERY AND HISTORY
  (article) (by Walter Galt)
  Adventure: May 1912

FROM HELL, HULL AND HALIFAX
  Everybody's: August 1913
  Pearson's (Br.): December 1913

FULL MOON (14-part serial)
  American Weekly: October 28, 1934
  Famous Fantastic Mysteries: February 1953
  Book: FULL MOON
  Book: THERE WAS A DOOR

THE GENTILITY OF IKEY BLUMENDALL
  Adventure: June 1914
  The Storyteller: (Br.): July 1914

THE GODS SEEM CONTENTED
   Argosy: September 15, 1934
   Book: MY BEST THRILLER

GOLDEN RIVER
   Adventure: January 1, 1929

THE GONER (by Walter Galt)
   Adventure: February 1912

THE GONER (by Talbot Mundy)
   Pall Mall (Br.): August 1912

GO TELL THE CZAR!
   Adventure: October 1914

THE GRAY MAHATMA
   Adventure: November 10, 1922
   Famous Fantastic Mysteries: December 1951
   Book: CAVES OF TERROR

GUARDED SECRETS (Quotation from THE DEVIL'S GUARD)
   Golden Book: December 1926

GULBAZ AND THE GAME
   Adventure: July 1914

GUNS OF THE GODS (5-part serial)
   Adventure: First March 1921
   Book: GUNS OF THE GODS

THE GUZZLER'S GRAND PRIX
   Adventure: May 1913

HAIL AND FAREWELL! (article)
   The Theosophical Path: September 1929

HEINIE HORNS INTO THE GAME
   Adventure: Mid-March 1919

THE HERMIT AND THE TIGER (article)
   American Cavalcade: November 1937

HIRA SINGH'S TALE (4-part serial)
   Adventure: Mid-October 1917
   Book: HIRA SINGH

HISTORY (verse)
   The Theosophical Path: August 1923

HO FOR LONDON TOWN! (4-part serial)
   Argosy All-Story: February 2, 1929
   Book: W.H.
   Book: THE QUEEN'S WARRANT

HONOR
   Adventure: November 1912

HOOKUM HAI
   Adventure: July 1913
   Book: TOLD IN THE EAST

HOPE (verse)
   The Theosophical Path: May 1924

HOPE (article)
   The Theosophical Path: May 1924

HOSTAGES TO LUCK
   Adventure: August 20, 1925
   Book: TROS OF SAMOTHRACE
   Book: AVENGING LIAFAIL

HOW IS A STORY WRITTEN (article) (excerpt from "Apology")
The Eclectic Theosophist, July-August 1980

THE "IBLIS" AT LUDD
Adventure: January 10, 1922

I HAVE RISEN (article)
The Theosophical Path: April 1929

IKEY HOLE'S LUCK
Cassell's Magazine of Fiction (Br.): December 1912

ILL WIND
Britannia & Eve (Br.): August 1935
The Grand (Br.): May 1937

IMPUDENCE IS ART
Britannia & Eve (Br.): May 1939

IN ALEPPO BAZAAR
Adventure: Mid-January 1920

IN OLD NARADA FORT
Adventure: February 15, 1929

IN A RIGHTEOUS CAUSE
Adventure: October 1913

THE INVISIBLE GUNS OF KABUL (5-part serial)
Adventure: October 1, 1929
Book: COCK O' THE NORTH
Book: GUP BAHADUR

IN WINTER QUARTERS
Adventure: September 1912
The Grand (Br.): December 1912
Newnes Summer Annual (Br.): November 2, 1916

I WILL AND I WILL NOT (article)
The Theosophical Path: August 1924

JACKSON TACTICS
Adventure: February 18, 1919

JANSEN AND THE JANSEN TWINS
Cavalier: August 1911

JERUSALEM (article)
The Theosophical Path: February 1923

A JUNGLE SAGE (article)
Adventure: March 15, 1932

KHUFU'S REAL TOMB
Adventure: October 10, 1922
Book: THE MYSTERY OF KHUFU'S TOMB

THE KING CAN DO NO WRONG (article)
The Theosophical Path: November 1923

THE KING IN CHECK
Adventure: July 10, 1922
Book: THE KING IN CHECK
Book: AFFAIR IN ARABY

KING DICK
Adventure: November 1914

KING, OF THE KHYBER RIFLES (9-part serial)
Everybody's: May 1916
Classics Illustrated (comic): May 1953, #107
Classics Illustrated (comic): (Br.), May 1954
Book: KING—OF THE KHYBER RIFLES
Book: KING, OF THE KHYBER RIFLES

KING OF THE WORLD (7-part serial)
Adventure: November 15, 1930
Book: JIMGRIM
Book: JIMGRIM SAHIB

KITTY BURNS HER FINGERS
The All-Story, July 1911

KITTY AND CUPID
The All-Story: December 1911

THE LADY AND THE LORD
The All-Story: June 1911

THE LAMA'S LAW (verse)
The Theosophical Path: April 1924

LANCING THE WHALE
Adventure: December 1914

THE LETTER OF HIS ORDERS
Adventure: September 1913

LION PARADISE (article)
Short Stories: August 10, 1932

THE LION OF PETRA
Adventure: March 20, 1922
Book: THE LION OF PETRA

THE LOST TROOPER
Adventure: May 30, 1922
Book: THE LOST TROOPER

LOVE AND WAR (by Walter Galt)
Adventure: November 1912

LOVE AND WAR (by Talbot Mundy)
  The Grand (Br.): October 1913

A LOW-VELDT FUNERAL (article)
  Adventure: February 1913

MacHASSAN AH
  Adventure: April 1915
  The Storyteller (Br.): June 1915
  Argosy (Br.): November 1930
  Book: TOLD IN THE EAST
  Book: THE VALIANT VIEW

MAKING £20,000
  McClure's: April 1913

THE MAN FROM POONCH
  Argosy: June 17, 1933
  Britannia & Eve (Br.): August 1933
  The Thriller (Br.): March 1935
  Book: THE VALIANT VIEW

THE MAN ON THE MAT
  Adventure: August 1, 1931

THE MAN WHO SAW
  Adventure: October 1912
  The Grand (Br.): March 1913

THE MARRIAGE OF MELDRUM STRANGE
  Adventure: October 10, 1923
  Book: THE MARRIAGE OF MELDRUM STRANGE

THE MAYA MYSTERY — YUCATAN (article)
  The Theosophical Path: December 1924

THE MESSENGER OF DESTINY (3-part serial)
Adventure: February 10, 1926
Book: TROS OF SAMOTHRACE
Book: THE PRAETOR'S DUNGEON

MILK OF THE MOON
The Passing Show (Br.): April 30, 1932
Argosy: September 17, 1938

MISCARRIAGE OF JUSTICE (article)
The Theosophical Path: March 1924

MOHAMMAD'S TOOTH
Adventure: December 10, 1923
Book: THE HUNDRED DAYS
Book: THE HUNDRED DAYS AND THE WOMAN AYISHA

MOSES AND MRS. AINTREE
Adventure: September 10, 1922

MYSTIC INDIA SPEAKS (article)
True Mystic Science: December 1938

A NEMESIS (verse)
The Theosophical Path: September 1923

THE NIGHT THE CLOCKS STOPPED
Adventure: March 1941

THE NINE UNKNOWN (5-part serial)
Adventure: March 20, 1923
Book: THE NINE UNKNOWN

NO NAME
Adventure: February 1915

NOTHING DOING (by Walter Galt)
Adventure: September 1914

OAKES RESPECTS AN ADVERSARY
Adventure: First December 1918

ODDS ON THE PROPHET
Short Stories: August 10, 1941

AN OFFER OF TWO TO ONE
The Scrap Book: November 1911

OH, JERUSALEM! (article)
The Delineator: April 1921

OLD UGLY FACE (3-part serial)
Maclean's (Can.): April 15, 1938
Book: OLD UGLY FACE

OM (6-part serial)
Adventure: October 10, 1924
Book: OM, THE SECRET OF AHBOR VALLEY

ONE EGYPTIAN NIGHT
Romance: May 1929

ONE YEAR LATER (by Walter Galt)
Adventure: February 1913

ON THE ROAD TO ALLAH'S HEAVEN
Adventure: December 1, 1928

ON TERMS
Adventure: March 1915
The Storyteller (Br.): July 1915

ON THE TRAIL OF SINDBAD THE SAILOR (article)
The Frontier: February 1925

ON THE TRAIL OF TIPPOO TIB (6-part serial)
Adventure: First May 1919
Book: THE IVORY TRAIL
Book: TREK EAST

OYEZ! (verse)
The Theosophical Path: July 1924

PATRIOTISM AND THE PLOW-TAIL (article)
Everybody's: January 1918

PAYABLE TO BEARER
Cavalier: December 28, 1912

THE PAYMENT OF QUINN'S DEBT
Adventure: August 1912

PETER FROM PARADISE BEND
The Crescent: May 1920

THE PHANTOM BATTERY
Adventure: August 1911
The Grand (Br.): September 1912

PIG-STICKING IN INDIA (article)
Adventure: April 1911

THE PILLAR OF LIGHT
Everybody's: December 1912
The Theosophical Path: September 1925 (2-part serial)
Book: THE VALIANT VIEW

THE PIPING DAYS OF PEACE
  Maclean's (Can.): June 1, 1937
  Book: MY BEST SPY STORY

THE PRINCESS
  Britannia & Eve (Br.): December 1936

PRISONERS OF WAR
  Adventure: June 10, 1925
  Book: TROS OF SAMOTHRACE
  Book: LUD OF LUNDEN, Chapters 1-7
  Book: AVENGING LIAFAIL, Chapters 8-11

PRIVATE MURDOCK'S G.C.M.
  Adventure: April 1913
  The Storyteller (Br.): July 1913

THE PURPLE PIRATE
  Adventure: August 15, 1935
  Book: PURPLE PIRATE

THE QUEEN — GOD BLESS HER!
  Adventure: May 1912
  London Magazine (Br.): January 1913
  The Boys Journal (Br.): Week ending October 4, 1913

QUITS!
  London Magazine: (Br.): June 1913

RABBIT
  Adventure: December 1912
  London Magazine (Br.): February 1913

RAMSDEN (5-part serial)
  Adventure: June 8, 1926
  Book: THE DEVIL'S GUARD
  Book: RAMSDEN

RANDOM REMINISCENCES OF AFRICAN BIG GAME (article)
The Saturday Evening Post: December 7, 1929

THE REAL RED ROOT
The Crescent: June 1919

THE RED FLAME OF ERINPURA
Adventure: January 1, 1927
Book: THE RED FLAME OF ERINPURA

RED SEA CARGO
Adventure: August 1933

THE RETURN OF BILLY BLAIN (by Walter Galt)
Adventure: November 1915

ROMAN HOLIDAY
Golden Fleece: October 1938

SAM BAGG OF THE GABRIEL GROUP (article)
The Storyteller (Br.): January 1916
The Saturday Evening Post: March 11, 1916
Argosy (Br.): April 1934

THE SECOND RING (by Walter Galt)
Adventure: June 1912

A SECRET SOCIETY
Adventure: August 10, 1922

SENTENCE OF DEATH
The Scrap Book: September 1911

THE SEVENTEEN THIEVES OF EL-KALIL
Adventure: February 20, 1922
Book: THE SEVENTEEN THIEVES OF EL-KALIL

THE SHRIEK OF DUN
   Adventure: First September 1919

SINCERITY (article)
   The Theosophical Path: April 1924

SINGLE-HANDED YACHTING (article)
   Adventure: July 1911

A SOLDIER AND A GENTLEMAN
   Adventure: January 1914

SOLOMON'S HALF-WAY HOUSE (4-part serial)
   Maclean's (Can.): August 15, 1934

SOME SAYINGS OF "HELL-FIRE" SMITH (article)
   Adventure: Mid-September 1919

THE SOUL OF A REGIMENT
   Adventure: February 1912
   The Grand (Br.): March 1912
   Adventure: April 1917
   The Theosophical Path: June 1925
   Adventure: November 1935
   Adventure: November 1940
   Adventure: November 1950
   Adventure: October 1954
   Short Stories (Br.): May 1981
   Book: THE SOUL OF A REGIMENT
   Book: THE VALIANT VIEW
   Book: ADVENTURE'S BEST STORIES
   Book: MY BEST ADVENTURE STORY

SPEED
   This Week: May 5, 1935
   Novel (Br.): November 1936

SPIRITUAL MAN IS ETERNAL: THERE ARE NO DEAD! (article)
(Also published as "The Art of Dying Daily")
The Theosophical Path: July 1929

SULPHUR'S NATIONAL
Strand (Br.): April 1913

T. C. ANSELL — ADVENTURER (article)
Adventure: June 1912

THE TEMPERING OF HARRY BLUNT
Adventure: December 1913
The Storyteller (Br.): July 1916

A TEMPORARY TRADE IN TITLES
Adventure: May 1915

THAT DARNED OLD NIGGER
New Magazine (Br.): June 1917

THE THINGS MEN FEAR (article)
Liberty: February 10, 1934

THREE HELIOS
Adventure: January 1913
Strand (Br.): July 1913

THE THUNDER DRAGON GATE (8-part serial)
American Weekly: January 24, 1937
Book: THE THUNDER DRAGON GATE

THE TOP OF THE LADDER (by Walter Galt)
Adventure: December 1912

A TRANSACTION IN DIAMONDS
The Scrap Book: February 1911
Corner Magazine (Br.): May 1926

THE TREACHEROUS ROAD (4-part serial)
This Week: August 15, 1937

TREASON
Adventure: January 10, 1923
Book: JUNGLE JEST

TROS OF SAMOTHRACE
Adventure: February 10, 1925
Book: TROS OF SAMOTHRACE
Book: LUD OF LUNDEN

TUCKER'S TONGUE (an anecdote)
Adventure: February 1916

A TUCKET OF DRUMS
Adventure: February 1, 1929

UNDER THE DOME OF THE ROCK
Adventure: December 10, 1921
Book: JIMGRIM AND ALLAH'S PEACE

UNIVERSAL (article)
The Theosophical Path: January 1924

UNIVERSAL BROTHERHOOD (article)
The Theosophical Path: September 1923

UNSUNG AS YET (verse)
The Theosophical Path: November 1925

VENGEANCE IS KITTY'S
The All-Story: August 1911

WATU (article)
Adventure: April 1, 1932

THE WHEEL OF DESTINY
Adventure: November 1, 1928
Book: THE GUNGA SAHIB

WHEN TRAILS WERE NEW (6-part serial)
Argosy All-Story: October 27, 1928
Book: WHEN TRAILS WERE NEW

WHITE TIGERS (2-part serial)
Adventure: August 1, 1932

THE WINDS OF THE WORLD (3-part serial)
Adventure: July 1915
Book: THE WINDS OF THE WORLD

W. MAYES — THE AMAZING (article)
Adventure: April 1912

THE WOLF OF THE PASS
All-Aces: May-June 1936

THE WOMAN AYISHA
Adventure: April 20, 1922
Book: THE HUNDRED DAYS AND THE WOMAN AYISHA
Book: THE WOMAN AYISHA

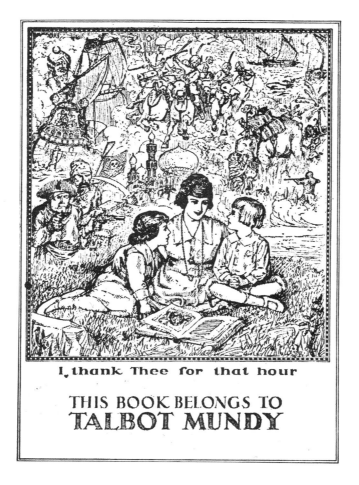

I thank Thee for that hour

THIS BOOK BELONGS TO
TALBOT MUNDY

Bookplate of Talbot Mundy.

The Black Watch, with Victor McLaglen and Myrna Loy in the starring roles, was the first (1928) of two movie versions of KING—OF THE KHYBER RIFLES. A 1953 production, with Tyrone Power in the role of King, was entitled *King of the Khyber Rifles*.

Adventure Intrigue Love Mystery

In An Unforgettable Moment...

he betrayed his trust and succumbed to the exotic, passionate allure of an Oriental beauty—inflamed with power — holding an empire in her hands...

A pulse-quickening breath-taking tale of mystery, intrigue, passion and conflict between a woman who ruled thousands of men and the one man who ruled her.

WILLIAM FOX

presents

this ALL-TALKING FOX MOVIETONE Melody-Melodrama with

VICTOR McLAGLEN

Myrna Loy, David Rollins, Roy D'Arcy, Cyril Chadwick, David Torrence

from Talbot Mundy's famous novel "King of the Khyber Rifles"

Dialog by James K. McGuinness

Staged by Lumsden Hare

JOHN FORD production

Watch for

"The BLACK WATCH"

THE JERUSALEM NEWS

from information supplied by
PETER BERRESFORD ELLIS

In 1919 a group of Americans led by Elizabeth M. McQueen organized to found an English-language newspaper for the American community in Jerusalem, Palestine. Among its supporters were Talbot Mundy and William Denison McCrackan (1864-1923), who was appointed editor. McCrackan was a journalist and author, and, until 1919, he had been associate editor of both the *Christian Science Journal* and *Christian Science Sentinel.* He was a friend of Mundy's who shared a deep interest in Christian Science with him, and Mundy tried, without success, to sell his publisher, Bobbs-Merrill, on a book by McCrackan, a memoir called AT HOME AND ABROAD. The English language newspaper, *The Jerusalem News,* was launched by McCracken on December 9, 1919. It was published daily, and consisted of a single sheet, tabloid size.

On January 3, 1920, Mundy sailed on the RMS Adriatic from New York to England. Travelling via London, Rome, and Alexandria, he reached Jerusalem on Thursday, February 5, 1920. The February 7, 1920 (Saturday) issue of *The Jerusalem News* reported:

> Mr Talbot Mundy, President of the Anglo-American Society of America, arrived in Jerusalem on February 5 by way of London and Rome. He brings glowing accounts of the evidence in England of the new spiritual growth that is following the war weariness. His impressions of London, seen after an absence of fifteen years, and of Italy in strike time, will appear in an early issue of *The Jerusalem News.*

In Jerusalem Mundy was to meet Mrs. Sarah T. Ames, a member of the American community engaged in charitable work. She returned to New York with him as his secretary. In 1924 they were married, settling at Point Loma, California.

SIGNED ARTICLES by TALBOT MUNDY in *The Jerusalem News:*

Monday, February 9, 1920. No. 52, Vol. 1
   "Italy in Strike Time"

Tuesday, February 10, 1920. No. 53, Vol. 1
   "England After the War" (1)
      also contains this note:
      A number of authentic animal stories have been written for us by Mr
      Talbot Mundy and will appear at intervals in this paper. Mr. Mundy
      has hunted big game from Rhodesia to Abyssinia and from Bombay
      to Assan. His experiences would fill many volumes, and his memory
      of men and animals met in many parts of the earth is a mine of absorb-
      ing interest.

Wednesday, February 11, 1920. No. 54, Vol. 1
   "England After the War" (2)

Thursday, February 12, 1920. No. 55, Vol. 1
   "England After the War" (3)

Friday, February 13, 1920. No. 56, Vol. 1
   "England After the War" (4)
   "Lord Dunsany" (1)

Saturday, February 14, 1920. No. 57, Vol. 1
   "Lord Dunsany" (2)

Monday, February 16, 1920. No. 59, Vol. 1
   " 'Mespot' "

Tuesday, February 17, 1920. No. 60, Vol. 1
   "America After the War" (1)

Wednesday, February 18, 1920. No. 61, Vol. 1
   "America After the War" (2)

Thursday, February 19, 1920. No. 62, Vol. 1
   "America After the War" (3)

Friday, February 20, 1920. No. 63, Vol. 1
   "America After the War" (4)

Monday, February 23, 1920. No. 66, Vol. 1
   "America After the War" (5)

Tuesday, March 2, 1920. No. 71, Vol. 1
   "Elizabeth" (East African Hunting Tale)

Saturday, March 6, 1920. No. 75, Vol. 1
   "Ready Rhino" (East African Hunting Tale)

Saturday, March 13, 1920. No. 81, Vol. 1
   "The American Rattlesnake"

Friday, March 26, 1920. No. 92, Vol. 1
   "Candles"

Saturday, March 27, 1920. No. 93, Vol. 1
   "Shooting Foxes"

Monday, April 5, 1920. No. 99, Vol. 1
   "Baboons"

An unsigned letter from Damascus, dated March 16, 1920 (with a by-line "Our Special Correspondent") appeared in the March 19, 1920 issue. It is in Mundy's style. In a letter to his publisher, W. C. Bobbs, dated April 19, 1920, Mundy wrote: "They let me go to Damascus recently to interview Feisal and his crew. Had a gorgeous time, and found out things that none of the regular correspondents know."

   Apart from the signed articles by Mundy, it is quite possible that a number of other unsigned pieces and some editorials came from his pen. In his letter to W. C. Bobbs of April 19, 1920, Mundy stated:

There has been serious rioting here of late*, which added to my labours, although it has compensated to some extent by making the paper a little more interesting. I imagine that someday the thing will grow into a valuable property. At present it doesn't pay its way, without any salary list. In fact, the only people who receive a salary are the typsetters, only one of whom knows a word of English. When there are more than a few words that don't need resetting on either page† after proof has been read twice, we give them a bonus. They walk out on us on Saints' Days, public holidays, when it rains, when it doesn't rain, when it snows, when they have cold feet, and when there's rioting. On other days they work if they feel like it. But the sheet comes out six days a week, and by steering the middle course between factions and mentioning no religious issues, offends everyone and pleases none.

He adds:

I hope to be relieved of my duties on this paper except insofar as I shall correspond for it wherever fortune leads me, sometime pretty soon, and then shall have lots of time for my own work, which is getting terribly behind.

The Jerusalem News ran from issue No. 1 (Tuesday, December 9, 1919) to issue No. 151 (Tuesday, June 8, 1920). In sending file copies to the British Museum, London, McCrackan wrote from Tamworth, New Hampshire on October 26, 1920:

The Jerusalem News was issued for six months during the last days of the British Military Administration in Palestine by a group of Americans as an act of friendship. Though it is a small sheet and is by no means free from typographical error, it is valuable as the only impartial newspaper issued in Jerusalem during this period, and in certain particulars contains authentic news of the time. With the coming of the Civil Administration in Palestine the paper ceased publication, as it was purely a war measure.

*On April 5 Martial Law had to be declared with a curfew from 6 P.M. to 6 A.M. by the British Military.
†The paper consisted of one sheet, two pages.

THE THEOSOPHICAL PATH

In the early 1920's, Talbot Mundy became a member of Katherine Tingley's theosophical community at Point Loma, California, where he was a regular contributor to *The Theosophical Path*, the journal of that organization.

1923

February	**Jerusalem** (article)
August	**History** (verse)
September	**A Nemesis** (verse)
	Universal Brotherhood (article)
October	**Brotherhood or League?** (article)
	Group Picture at International Theosophical Headquarters, Point Loma, California (includes Talbot Mundy)
November	**The King Can Do No Wrong** (article)
December	**The Turning Tide:** Book reviews by Talbot Mundy of *Men Like Gods* by H. G. Wells and *Legends of Smokeover* by L. P. Jacks.

1924

January	**Universal** (article)
February	**Book Review** by Talbot Mundy of *Mother Nature* by William J. Long.
March	**The Miscarriage of Justice** (article)
March	**Letter:** "Talbot Mundy Says San Diego Has Opportunity to Set Pace for This Glorious West Coast." (Reprinted from the *San Diego Union*, February 4, 1924.)
	Critique by Talbot Mundy of Katherine Tingley's Greek Theater Production of "The Eumenides" by Aeschylus. (Reprinted from the *San Diego Union*, March 23, 1924.)
April	**Sincerity** (article)
	The Lama's Law (verse)
	Eastern Proverb (verse)

	Letter: "Well-known writer (Talbot Mundy) predicts brilliant career for San Diego artist (Maurice Braun). (Reprinted from the *San Diego Union*, March 2, 1924.)
May	**Hope** (verse)
	Hope (article)
June	**Fata Virumque Cano** (verse)
	Blackmail (article)
July	**Oyez!** (verse)
	Another's Duty Is Full of Danger (article)
	Review: Talbot Mundy Reviews Another Performance of "The Eumenides." (Reprinted from the *San Diego Union*, June 4, 1924.)
	Address by Talbot Mundy at White Lotus Day Celebration.
July	**I Will and I Will Not** (article)
	Chant (verse)
December	**The Maya Mystery — Yucatan** (article)
	Review: *Om, the Secret of Ahbor Valley*, An Appreciation, by G. d. Purucker.
	Photograph: Talbot Mundy
	From the Book of the Sayings of Tsiang Samdup
	About Talbot Mundy: (Miscellaneous Headquarters Notes).

1925

January	**An Answer to Correspondents** (article)
	Book Review by Talbot Mundy of Katherine Tingley's *Wine of Life*.
February	**As to Writing and Reading** (article)
	Talbot Mundy on "Om" (extract from "The Camp-Fire," published in *Adventure*, October 10, 1924.)
March	**Extract** from Talbot Mundy's preface to *Wine of Life* by Katherine Tingley. (Reprinted from the *San Diego Union*, February 6, 1925.)
April	**As to Success and Failure** (article)
	About Talbot Mundy: "Talbot Mundy's *Om* much appreciated."
May	**A Beginner's Concept of Theology** (article)
June	**The Soul of a Regiment** (fiction)
July	**Extracts from an Address** by Talbot Mundy to the State Disabled Veterans and War-Mothers of California.

September	**The Pillar of Light,** part 1 (fiction)
	Tribute to Katherine Tingley on her birthday, July 6, 1925, by by Talbot Mundy.
October	**The Pillar of Light,** part 2 (fiction)
November	**Unsung as Yet** (verse)
December	**As to Capital Punishment** (article)

1927

January	**Apology** (article)
April	**Announcement** of Katherine Tingley's proposed 1926 European Tour, to be accompanied by Talbot Mundy and others. Contains biographical sketch of Mundy.
September	**Talbot Mundy** toasts Katherine Tingley on her birthday, July 6, 1926.

1927

| July | **Tribute to Fred J. Dick** by Talbot Mundy. |

1928

| January | **Extract of Speech** by Talbot Mundy at the Reception for Colonel Arthur L. Conger, November 4, 1927. |
| May | **About Talbot Mundy:** Two paragraphs citing Mundy in article "The Divinity of Nature in the Art of Maurice Braun" by Reginald Poland. |

1929

April	**I Have Risen** (article)
July	**Spiritual Man Is Eternal: There Are No Dead** (article)
September	**Hail and Farewell!** (article)

Inscription pasted to the title page of Katherine Tingley's copy of OM — THE SECRET OF AHBOR VALLEY.

November, 1924

To Madame Katherine Tingley,
   Lomaland

Dear Leader,
   This book was written in your house while I was your guest. What wisdom it contains was learned from you, and its unwisdom is my own. Without your teaching, patience, and encouragement I could not have "imagined" either the wise old Lama or his chela. Be this, therefore, a written record of my gratitude and obligation to you.

Talbot Mundy

Printed by permission of Point Loma Publications, Inc., San Diego, California.

THE NEW YORK TIMES

Talbot Mundy was represented in *The New York Times* with the following articles and letters:

May 25, 1919 — "America as Protector of Armenia"

December 6, 1928 — "Triumvirate of Mayors"

June 30, 1929 — "An Author's Characters"

February 11, 1930 — "The Result of Cynicism"

Note: "An Author's Characters," written at the time of the release of the movie *The Black Watch* (based on Mundy's book KING—OF THE KHYBER RIFLES), is a revealing article about Yasmini and the Khyber Pass.